Tales from EUTOPIA

Thirteen Short Stories

Llewellyn Mark Jones

Copyright © 2020 Llewellyn Mark Jones.

All rights reserved. No part of this book may be used or reproduced by any means, graphic, electronic, or mechanical, including photocopying, recording, taping or by any information storage retrieval system without the written permission of the author except in the case of brief quotations embodied in critical articles and reviews.

Archway Publishing books may be ordered through booksellers or by contacting:

Archway Publishing
1663 Liberty Drive
Bloomington, IN 47403
www.archwaypublishing.com
844-669-3957

Because of the dynamic nature of the Internet, any web addresses or links contained in this book may have changed since publication and may no longer be valid. The views expressed in this work are solely those of the author and do not necessarily reflect the views of the publisher, and the publisher hereby disclaims any responsibility for them.

Any people depicted in stock imagery provided by Getty Images are models, and such images are being used for illustrative purposes only. Certain stock imagery © Getty Images.

Scripture taken from the New King James Version® Copyright © 1982 by Thomas Nelson. Used by permission. All rights reserved.

ISBN: 978-1-4808-9907-0 (sc)
ISBN: 978-1-4808-9906-3 (hc)
ISBN: 978-1-4808-9908-7 (e)

Library of Congress Control Number: 2020925063

Print information available on the last page.

Archway Publishing rev. date: 12/18/2020

Tales from Eutopia is a work of fiction. If readers see resemblances to things or people in reality, then the writer and audience share common, coincidental experiences. The purpose of writing these short stories is to present written art for consideration and entertainment.

This collection of stories could not have existed without the support of Rema Parchment MacLean, Dave Signal, Megan Mutler, Susan Jones, and Gerard Gill. I am grateful for their wisdom, guidance, patience, and encouragement. Gerard, your kindness has no limits.

The creative process requires inspiration and alternative perspectives. Fiction imitates and echoes reality, also twisting, reshaping, refining, and displaying it through a lens. These stories have been fun to form.

This book is dedicated to Peter Fairburn, my teacher, mentor, encourager, supporter, and friend. You are missed.

Llewellyn Mark Jones
Glen Tay (Perth), Ontario, Canada
May 26, 2020

A little learning is a dangerous thing;
Drink deep, or taste not the Pierian spring:
There shallow draughts intoxicate the brain,
And drinking largely sobers us again.

—Alexander Pope, "An Essay on Criticism"

My brethren, let not many of you become teachers, knowing that we shall receive a stricter judgment.

—James 3:1 (NKJV)

QUOTED FROM THE EUTOPIA BOARD WEBSITE:

Eutopia School Division does not have problems; it has opportunities. As with many other school boards, it serves diverse community members with differing opinions on the scope, operation, and purpose of education. Providing wide, deep, and meaningful learning possibilities for students is its goal. Eutopia School Division is a world leader in disseminating the latest advances in scholastic practice.

Every parent has also been a student. Those parents have accumulated in their scholastic lifetimes positive and negative experiences with students, teachers, schools, and administrators. Thus, they are educational experts. Add that they want their children to be successful. This should be helpful to everyone. If only ...

TABLE OF CONTENTS

Staring Truth 1
The Deacon 12
Gifted.. 18
Inclusion 27
The Lonely Beat on Simcoe Street 39
Dramatic Irony.. 46
Kingdoms 55
What's a Foot?... 64
Breaking Bull Brown 72
Indulgence 84
Reunion.. 93
The New Girl 101
Group Work 111

STARING TRUTH

IN SEPTEMBER 1962 in New Orleans, Louisiana, Herbert Fraser Junior started kindergarten at Claiborne Public School. He was ready, even looking forward to it. He and his friend, Bubba, were in the same class. To their mothers, Herbert and Bubba going to school together seemed like a long-awaited and overdue idea. However, the mothers had immediate sympathy for the boys' teacher, Mrs. Hart.

"Lord, have mercy on Mrs. Hart," Bubba's mother said to Herbert's mom. "She's got her hands full."

Bordering that New Orleans Baptist Theological Seminary neighbourhood, Claiborne Public School incorporated many children from the campus where their fathers studied. On seminary property and environs, children collected and shared many experiences, including raising chicks, baby ducks, hatched turtles and alligators, kittens, and puppies. They had freedom to explore—Bubba and Junior even more so. Their searches sometimes landed them in trouble.

Their mothers appreciated that Mrs. Hart had experience on her side. She managed her classroom with precision and impressive organisation. "That woman has those kids so busy that our boys don't even have a second to think about trouble," Bubba's mother shared with Mrs. Fraser. "Mrs. Hart talks to each student daily about things going on in their lives. You should visit the classroom, Louise. Herbert Junior behaves himself. You'd be quite proud."

Every morning, Mrs. Hart's students recited the Pledge of Allegiance while holding small American flags in their left hands, placing their right hands over their hearts, and staring at a picture of President John F. Kennedy. Students learned and practised patriotism.

Mrs. Hart established a quiet time, one of the routines in kindergarten that allowed her to speak personally to each student. Lights went out, and students took turns being the Sandman. A little bucket with imaginary sleeping dust became the prop by which each Sandman with a small shovel spread slumber. Students coveted the role. Herbert Junior never slept, but he remained silent. When Mrs. Hart and Herbert spoke, it was in whispers. Their first Sandman conversation started with Herbert Junior telling Mrs. Hart that his father had injured his back at work.

"He was lifting plastic rolls at work, and it really hurt him."

Mrs. Hart responded with a quick hug. "The poor man. Tell him I'm sorry."

Junior smiled.

On the second day, Herbert Junior said, "Dogs attacked my dad yesterday. It was scary."

Mrs. Hart asked with concern, "You were there?"

"Yes, and I couldn't do anything. They scared me."

"Did they hurt you?"

"No. They just scared me a lot. They hurt Dad."

"How's your father now?"

"Oh, he's fine."

"That's awful. I'm so glad both of you are doing well." Mrs. Hart patted Herbert twice on his back. He smiled with appreciation, and she moved on to the next student.

On the third day, Junior revealed, "Dad breaked his legs in a car accident."

"That's awful! Is he okay?"

"Oh, he's okay. He'll be better soon," Herbert Junior responded. Again, Mrs. Hart gave him a hug.

When Louise Fraser visited the classroom a few days later, Mrs. Hart said, "I heard your husband's not doing so well."

Louise appeared surprised. "No, he's fine."

"His back?" Mrs. Hart pointed to her own back.

"Oh, yes. Herbert works two jobs; in the day he sells cars, and at night he works at the plastics factory. Then, of course, he has studies at the seminary as well. He came home in considerable pain after one of his shifts at about two o'clock in the morning. Herbert doesn't like to show weakness, but the noise from his pain woke Junior. Herbert has taken plenty of aspirin and rested for a few days now, just reading. He went to work today to his day job," Louise explained.

"And his broken legs?" Mrs. Hart inquired. Louise looked dumbfounded, so Mrs. Hart clarified, "From a car accident?"

"Herbert Senior was hit from behind by another car, but it was just a fender bender." Louise paused. "Now that I think about it, Junior did have a nightmare about it that same night. He dreamed that his father broke his legs."

With relief, Mrs. Hart commented, "I'm glad to hear your husband's back is improving. Junior was so worried. And what about your husband's dog bites?"

"Dog bites?" Silence followed. Louise could not fathom her question. Then she smiled. "Oh. You mean another one of Junior's nightmares. He thought his father and he were being attacked by a pack of dogs just outside of the town house. It took an hour to calm him before he returned to sleep. It felt very real to him." Louise played unconsciously with her purse and smiled. "Herbert Junior's father is just fine, thank you."

"Junior has quite an imagination," Mrs. Hart commented.

"Yes, I suppose he does," Mrs. Fraser replied.

That evening, as they sat down to watch television together on the couch, Mrs. Hart told her husband, Fred, a commander of the New Orleans Police Department, about Junior's stories. "What do you think about Junior, Fred?"

"Honey, he sounds like trouble. Keep an eye on that boy."

"He's sweet, Fred. He means no harm."

"Liars are always liars. You can't change the colours on a skunk."

In October during one of Sandman's visits, Herbert Junior told Mrs. Hart about his neighbour, Dan Dodge, a theology student. "After I heard the gunshots, I went outside. Dan shot five black squirrels with a pistol. He held them by the tails with one hand, and he had the pistol in the other. He was gonna skin them for dinner."

"Here in New Orleans? At the seminary?"

"There are lots of squirrels in those big trees. He shot up in the trees to get them. He's a good shooter."

"Did the police come?"

"No." Herbert Junior seemed surprised by her query.

Mrs. Hart had another question for Junior. "You didn't dream this, did you?"

Junior smiled before he whispered, "No. I wanted to see him skin the squirrels, but Mom said I had to come in for dinner."

"Your mother knew about this?"

"I think so. She waved to Dan when he went into his house with the squirrels. Then she told me to sit down for dinner."

Mrs. Hart abandoned her interrogation and lost herself in her thoughts. Rest time ended early.

When Mrs. Hart shared that story with her husband, the commander spoke, "No laws broken if no complaints come in. Come on, honey; this is the South. People are law-abiding, especially on the seminary. God-fearing people, they are. Even the boy wasn't bothered by it. Nothing to worry about, honey."

Later that month, an argument between Bubba and Junior broke out in the classroom. Other students gathered around, and Mrs. Hart feared a fight would commence. She got there in time to limit their conflict to only words. When she asked Bubba what was wrong, he replied, "Junior stole my bicycle."

"Is this true, Herbert Fraser Junior?" his teacher inquired.

"Kinda. I was late for school. Bubba left his bike on his lawn, so I took it to get here. I left it outside by the corner. I forgot to tell Bubba."

Barbara, a classmate, spoke. "I told Bubba that Junior took his bike." She wore her loyalty to Bubba well as she leaned into him. "Junior shouldn't have done that."

Mrs. Hart took charge. "I agree, Barbara. Now, Junior, you go outside and bring that bicycle inside this classroom before someone else steals it."

After school, Mrs. Hart phoned Mrs. Fraser.

"Thanks for making me aware of this. Junior's father and I will be disciplining him, rest assured."

"I wanted to make sure you knew," Mrs. Hart replied.

"Those boys are quite the pair. Just the other day, they were playing with matches in a tepee. It burned down. They tried to put the fire out themselves. It's fortunate that they didn't get badly burned, just slightly on their hands. I don't know what gets into these boys, but Herbert is determined to get it out of Junior."

Mrs. Hart wondered what that meant, but if more discipline was required, she supported it. "Oh, it's not easy, Mrs. Fraser. I've seen it again and again over many years, including with my own children. There's a natural curiosity on their part, but knowing right from wrong and having common sense hasn't happened yet. They're too young. But I must say, your boy has a good heart. For the most part, he behaves for me. Bubba does too. I'm delighted to be their teacher."

Mrs. Fraser smiled when she hung up the phone.

"Can I go over to Dan Dodge's house to watch TV?" Junior asked. "He said I could watch anytime."

Mrs. Fraser's smile left her. "No privileges for you, Herbert Fraser Junior. You stole Bubba's bicycle today!" Louise also considered all the disturbing news lately in the papers and radio. She didn't want him to think about nuclear war, and neither did she. His actions required serious introspection and little else. "Wait till your father gets home."

Louise added that last comment with experiential assurance that she would have no trouble from Junior for the rest of the afternoon. Junior appeared uncomfortable. "Stealing a bicycle! What were you thinking? Haven't we raised you to do the right things?" She paused and then returned to preparing dinner. "Now, go play nicely with your brother, David, while I get supper ready."

Commander Fred Hart commended his wife on her handling of the situation. "That Junior learned a good lesson today because of you, and his father will deal with him as fathers should. There may be hope for Junior," he said as he swallowed his baked ribs. "Lovely meal tonight, honey."

That November, Bubba and Junior lied about their age to gain use of the gymnasium on campus. Their favourite activity was climbing ropes right to the ceiling. That skill added to their existing ability to easily climb all kinds of trees. Mrs. Hart heard about their fibs. "You have to be seven years old to use that gym," she scolded. "Now, I know you boys are big for your age, but you put everyone else there in a bad position. You wait until you're seven before you use that gym."

"Are you going to tell my parents?" asked Junior.

"Yes. And Bubba's parents too."

"Mrs. Hart, please," Junior protested.

"You hear me, boys. Telling the truth at all times is extremely important. You need to learn that lesson. Your parents are going to help me with administering that lesson." In reaction, Junior unconsciously started to rub the left side of his buttocks with his left hand.

Fred Hart commented that evening, "That boy and truth couldn't find each other even if they were tied to each other."

From that point, Mrs. Hart, with support from Bubba and Junior's parents, wielded benevolent authority over the boys. Yet the boys harboured no resentment toward their parents or Mrs. Hart. In class, they helped her and cooperated with classmates well into the new year. Supportive leadership with their peers flowed from them. Mrs. Hart considered her teaching career and concluded that perhaps this had been the best-behaved class she had ever taught. For her, that meant students could learn more, and that possibility enthused her.

Weekly, Barbara's mother volunteered to play piano so Mrs. Hart could lead her students in singing. On a rainy March day, as she wandered the class during their choral exercises, she listened to each student's voice. At the end of the school day, Mrs. Hart asked Junior to stay for a few minutes.

After the other students left, she instructed, "Come with me to the piano, Junior." She sat on the piano stool and began to play.

"You can play the piano, Mrs. Hart? I didn't know," Junior commented.

"Barbara's mother is a big help. Because of her, I can listen to each child's voice when he or she sings. I've been listening to yours for a few months now, and I believe you can sing better than you do." Junior lowered his head. "Come on, now; don't be sad. You have a beautiful voice if you would just let it come out. That growly bear sound of yours isn't very musical, but I know there's one lovely singing voice waiting to take over. Now, let me hear you sing the National Anthem." Mrs. Hart began to play and sing. Herbert Junior joined her with his usual guttural utterance.

"Not that voice, Herbert Fraser Junior. Think higher. Try to make your voice match the notes I'm playing." She switched to playing the melody only. Then with some surprise on Junior's part, his singing began to match the notes she played. He smiled. She glanced at him and smiled with him. She resumed playing the anthem in harmony. When they finished, Mrs. Hart patted him on the back. "That's the voice I knew you had in you. Well done. Let's hear that voice from now on. You can go home now." Junior's smile remained when he skipped his way out of the classroom, down the hall, and out into the schoolyard.

"He'll be a good singer in jail, that boy. Singin' like a bird," Commander Fred Hart joked to his wife that evening. "The Birdman of Alcatraz."

In early June, Mr. and Mrs. Fraser informed the school that the family would be moving back to Canada at the end of the month. Junior's school record would be sent to Grey Park Public School in Fort William, Ontario, where Junior would start grade 1 in September. "That's straight north on Highway 61, and 61 ends in Fort William," Herbert Senior explained to Mrs. Hart and the principal, who were unfamiliar with Canadian geography.

Mrs. Hart held a party for her students on the last day of school before the summer break. Her students' excitement could barely be contained. Many students had gifts for Mrs. Hart, and she accepted them with hugs. Bubba brought in a brown box a baby chick for her. Junior gave her maple candy from Ontario, Canada. Despite the brave façade that their kindergarten teacher attempted to keep, tears betrayed her. The good news was that all students would be in the school next year, so she would see them regularly—except Herbert Fraser Junior. She wanted to have a special goodbye with him after everyone else had left.

"What's it like in Fort William, Junior?"

"Dad says there's lots of fish there—big fish." Junior extended his hands as far as possible apart. "He said we could go fishing a lot."

"What will you miss from here, Junior?"

"Lake Pontchartrain. It's the best place. And I'll miss the beignets at the café. And Bubba. And you. And … can I tell you something? It's about President Kennedy."

With that, Mrs. Hart's curiosity triggered. "What's that, Junior?"

"There's a man that wants to kill him."

"A man who wants to kill President Kennedy?"

Junior hesitated. "His name is Lee."

"How do you know this, Junior?"

"I saw him at Lake Pontchartrain. He was giving papers to people. Some people threw the papers away. Some people argued with him. They called him a commist. What's a commist, Mrs. Hart?"

"A communist?"

"I think so. He yelled at them about something called Cuba."

"How do you know that he wants to kill President Kennedy?"

"He told me. He was angry. When the other people left, he told me that. He wanted to give me a paper, but I told him I don't know how to read yet. He said someone should shoot President Kennedy. Then he said that maybe he would take his gun and shoot the president. That's not right, Mrs. Hart. President Kennedy is good."

"Yes, he's a good man, Junior. Did you tell your parents about this man named Lee?"

"No. David fell and cut his knee, so Mom helped him. Dad was at work."

Mrs. Hart assured Junior, "Thanks for telling me. I will speak with my husband, who is a police officer. We want to protect President Kennedy. Did he say he would kill President Kennedy to anyone else?"

"No. Just me. We were alone." Junior paused. A look of desperation penetrated his teacher's conscience. "Mrs. Hart, can you stop him from hurting President Kennedy?"

When she informed Commander Fred Hart about Junior's conversation, he responded after lowering his newspaper, "That's the boy who lies and burns things, right?"

"Well, yes, but he's been much better behaved lately. I take the threat to our president seriously, Fred." With her most compelling eye contact and facial expression of expectation, Mrs. Hart continued, "I hope you do too."

Fred Hart had seen that look before. "I'll look into it, honey," he promised. He sensed a small smile from his wife, who released her glare. He felt safe enough to raise the paper and continue reading.

A few days later after work, Commander Fred Hart in their kitchen reported to his wife. "There's been some guy handing out leaflets on Cuba in a few places around New Orleans. People call to complain about it, but by the time we get there, he's gone. We'll find him. The pamphlets mention an A. J. Hidell. That's most likely the man. There's nobody by the name of Lee. As far as wanting to shoot Kennedy, we talked to the complainants, but nobody other than your little liar heard a threat to kill Kennedy." He poked with a wooden ladle at the okra that rested inside a pot on the stove.

His wife slapped his hand. "No sampling before dinner." Fred let go of the ladle. "He's not a liar. Junior has an active imagination, but he was very concerned about the safety of our president. He trusted me to get to the bottom of it. I told him that you are a police officer, so he seemed satisfied that you would look into it. You have, so thank you, Fred."

On a grey, windy November 22, 1963, in Fort William, at the end of his school day, Herbert Fraser Junior walked toward home while his fingers unconsciously brushed the chain-link fence that bordered Grey Park Public School. A classmate, Jonathan, ran back toward the school and stopped in front of Junior. "Someone shot President Kennedy!" he announced. The two boys looked at each other without talking. Junior absorbed what he heard. "It's on the TV," Jonathan reported.

"Lee did it," Junior proclaimed. He then ran home, bolted past his mother, and turned on the television. "Lee shot President Kennedy, Mom."

"What?" she asked. She wiped her hands on her apron and sat on the chesterfield. Junior's brother, David, watched television with them, but he soon returned to playing with his Tinker Toy collection. The news shocked and upset Louise Fraser, so she found reason to return to the kitchen. "I need to get supper ready," she offered. "Your father should be home soon."

Tears flowed from Junior's face, but he refused to make any sound. Mrs. Hart taught him how to sing. She could do almost anything. At the moment he considered singing was too close to sobbing. He wondered how Mrs. Hart's husband could have let Lee kill President Kennedy.

THE DEACON

I WORKED WITH SEVERAL colourful characters throughout my career, but my first school seemed to have the most. The jocks weren't typical. They loved the great outdoors, including daredevil, white-water canoeing. They could be led by one English teacher, their drinking buddy, who persuaded them to read W. P. Kinsella short stories. As a result, they formed an informal book club. They also could be steered by one geeky social studies teacher who invested in frozen bull semen, making the staffroom a trade centre and an uncomfortable place for some.

There was a female rancher who, as a widow, entered teaching later in life. Her subject was business. Still a ranch owner, she fought and defeated every corporation and government agency that dared threaten her land and animals. She had great spunk, determination, insight, and wisdom, but I most respected her love of teaching kids. Another talented colleague made enthralling mosaics with multi-toned, interlocking pieces of cedar, usually of landscapes and animals. His abrupt death, I suspect, resulted from breathing cedar dust.

One senior high teacher who also coached rugby had passions for many things. In younger years, he had red hair, so when he lost it, he shaved his head. Nevertheless, when he lost his temper, his natural colour fully returned everywhere hair used to be. His social studies colleague with a legal background from Jamaica complemented the rugby coach when arguing tag-team style over points with the principal during staff meetings. Because the principal could also turn red, the legal approach garnered more success.

The principal also had flare. He was an American veteran from the Italian campaign in World War II, and unlike most veterans, he told war stories—lots of them, and they were never short. Most storage spaces in the school were full of foolscap, which he bought in bulk and sold to other schools for a profit to benefit our school. Clever and as entrepreneurial as it was, room to stow anything could not be found.

One secretary may have emulated Loni Anderson's character, Jennifer Marlowe, from the television show *WKRP in Cincinnati* because she regularly worked on her nails, hair, and appearance—without Jennifer Marlowe's talents. She accomplished little office work, but like Jennifer, she had connections that one did not cross or question. Despite a lack of productivity, her employment remained secure.

One guidance teacher also taught English. Her family's notoriety followed her. Her father and brother wrestled professionally, and she provided free tickets to wrestling for her students as rewards for their good work and behaviour. That made her popular.

Lately, memories return from those days in my early career. Now, some friends say that because I actively search for obituaries, I possess morbid curiosity. There's some truth in that. Let me clarify. I truly don't like obits; reading them reminds me of my own mortality. However, since relocation elsewhere and retirement some distance from Eutopia, I search for death notices about former colleagues from Eutopia School District. Over the years, I learned too late about some of their deaths. It became difficult to pay respects.

Even more upsetting are the deaths of former students, especially when I was teaching. Those are tragic. The loss of human potential gnaws at hope. It's unrealistic to expect that people leave this earth in the same chronological order that they entered it, but that's how I think it should be. Call me an idealist. Better yet would be to keep contact with all former students and colleagues through social media, so that their passing is known more immediately. However, that doesn't happen. Still, for a while, we shared time and experiences together.

The Deacon died five years ago. I learned about it last week on the Internet. He was a likeable but odd fellow, not as colourful as most of our colleagues at that school, and full of contradiction, like us all. I commuted to and from work with him and two other car mates in my first year of teaching. He taught art. His retirement wasn't close enough; patience for educational and school politics left him years earlier. In the car, although we knew he could laugh with jolliness, we endured his complaints against the guidance department that sent unmotivated junior high students into his already oversized classroom. There weren't even enough desks in the classroom. Supplies were threadbare. There wasn't enough storage space for students to place with security their works in progress. He underwent moments of joy in his work with rarity. Senior students with artistic talents, dedication, and maturity made his days tolerable.

He said to me once, "Malcolm, this profession will chew you up and spit you out." That did not encourage me as a young teacher. In fact, that's partly why I stopped driving with him. I vowed that I would never be like that. I saw too many other teachers in their last five years who gave misery a bad name. Conversely, I found principals in their last five years to be excellent. They could not be intimidated. They knew how to manipulate the bureaucracy for the school's needs. That was one of many reasons why I became an administrator toward the end of my career. I too could do what was right rather than some of the ridiculous things the system expected.

One activity outside of school that gave Clair (Sinclair) Cerf, the Deacon, happiness was planning for retirement. As an active lay leader in his Anglican church, his service to God, his community, and all humanity revealed the pleasure it provided him. He sought to move from lay leader to deacon, which required some theological training. This would lead to graduation and ordination within his denomination. As carpoolers, we enjoyed Clair's brighter and more hopeful topic of conversation, so we encouraged him in his pursuit. He suffered one setback when the denomination rejected his first attempt to become a deacon. For about two weeks afterward, he remained quiet. His belly laughs ceased. We encouraged him to try again, and he did with success a few months later. There would be life after education.

In my second year of teaching, my wife and I built a house. We hired trades to do the work we could not do. Almost at its completion for occupancy, we learned through radio, television, and print media that a young woman who lived a few houses away in our new neighbourhood was murdered. Someone found her body in a countryside snowbank, burned by diesel fuel. Daily new details of the murder repeated in all local media. In our small community of Eutopia, this created terror and fear. Distrust produced isolation. Everyone became a suspect. Neighbours with apprehensions, however tenuous, reported them. Police were desperate for clues and searched people's garbage for evidence. The press, in particular one tabloid, hounded the widower. Rumours and judgement without reasoning, trust, and compassion prevailed. For that Christmas, peace and goodwill abandoned Eutopia.

In late January, a second, amplified shock horrified our small community. One of our grade 12 students, while she was working alone one evening at her part-time job in a convenience store, disappeared. Her burnt body emerged, like the first murder, in a rural snowbank a few days later. The morning after media reported the identity of her body, our principal called a staff meeting before classes began.

It was a staggering start to our day. We learned that our principal had contacted the murdered student's family to communicate the school community's sorrow with this tragic loss. The guidance department had prepared as best it could for the expected fallout of grieving friends and other students. The staff received advice on dealing with anguish and how to assist students in crisis. For a few days of expected chaos, Eutopia Junior and Senior High School would be grieving. An assembly of the entire school would occur after attendance had been taken.

I knew of the student, Vicky Golden, but hadn't taught her. It would be difficult for me to speak specifically about her to students. Nevertheless, students also lived in a tight-knit community. Whether or not a child in grade 7 knew the victim, a grade 12, mattered little. Not many students had experiences with death, so the concept could be frightening. These murders shocked everyone. Teacher's college did not prepare us for this.

At the hushed assembly, the principal, student council president, and guidance head spoke. What surprised me was the introduction by the principal of Clair Cerf, the Deacon, as the main speaker. Dressed in a simple clerical robe, Mr. Cerf addressed with palpable compassion all those numbed, injured individuals at the gathering. I don't remember any time in my career when students required no reminders about what good conduct should be. They behaved admirably.

The Deacon began with this: "I don't understand evil." Neither do I. Neither do students and children. His talk displayed careful crafting, knowing his audience well. Its length was not too long and not too short. Clair Cerf escorted us through grieving for Vicky, a student whom many loved. She was part of everyone there whether or not we knew her. In every student and staff member, a little piece of us died by murder. If we didn't understand evil, we knew now it existed, and it affected us all. Nonetheless, the Deacon encouraged all of us to resolve that evil would not defeat us. Faith in truth and good and others, hope for a brighter future, and love for all people would render evil powerless. Clair Cerf transported us to a tranquil shore where fog was lifting as sunshine warmed our faces. We discerned that despite their ethereal nature, peace and healing could be grasped.

Clair delivered us from evil. As a messenger, he dispensed peace during a tense time in Eutopia. A few short weeks later, police had arrested two men who had committed those murders. That made news, as did their trial and subsequent sentencing. The media continued to hound the widower and Vicky's family for comment. After two years in jail, one of the murderers committed suicide. To this day, the other one remains remorseless, unrepentant, and unapologetic. His requests for parole continue to be denied. Evil exists, but it belongs in a jail cell for longer than life.

Somehow in a short time, Eutopia returned to normal. Even with changes, the resilience that the Deacon encouraged took hold. Vicky Golden's murder no longer was about the power of evil. Her tragedy, although still felt today, seemed more a symbolic triumph over malevolence. Justice, as inadequate and flawed as it can be, allowed fear to fade and daily joy to return. Clair's inspired stirring for community faith, hope, and love brought us through that horrific time.

Students have preferences for teachers; they connect with some and have aversions to others. Like students, teachers have unique personalities. Their devotion to teaching, students, and subject matter meld with their characters, and from that time together teachers are capable of affecting forever the lives of those they teach. A few students have told me that I have accomplished that. As a colleague, I regret not telling Clair what he did for me at that moment.

Clair Cerf's obituary told me that his wife had died ten years earlier. He volunteered in several organisations, and he enjoyed time with his daughters and their families. He had roles as deacon, minister, and veterans' chaplain during life after teaching. It's what he wanted, and I have no doubt his presence and work among the faithful would be a blessing to them all. If only I had made contact with him to inform him before his death how meaningful his guidance, leadership, and ministry had been during that sickening time. Maybe he already knew it.

GIFTED

2019-02-19

TODAY IS THE first day of my single credit, grade twelve co-op placement. I want a career working with people who have developmental disabilities, so this is a good assignment for me. Ms. Fine is the teacher in charge of this senior associated class. As I become more familiar with routines and the students here, I can take on roles assigned to me. One of the educational assistants, Ms. Goodfellow, showed me software on classroom computers, so she suggested that I become familiar with programs that the students use. I was also introduced to everyone. Students greeted me warmly. That period went quickly!

2019-02-20

Vice Principal Featherstone let us know about a fire drill this period. One of the students, Fortune, reacts violently to loud noises. That's why Mr. Featherstone warned us about the fire drill. Ms. Goodfellow, Ms. Mosca, Fortune, and I had to get our winter clothing on and take Fortune outside to the Eutopia Public Library next door to the school. Fortune opened and closed newspapers and looked at Harry Potter pictures on a computer. When Mr. Featherstone contacted us over the walkie-talkie about completion of the fire drill, we returned just in time for the class to go to their buses.

2019-02-21

I helped with preparation of snack time. The students and staff sit around joined tables and take a break together. Normally, it's at the end of the period before my co-op time. I help with clean-up daily.

One student's name is Patrick. He's friendly and full of questions, mostly personal. Ms. Fine says I don't have to answer them, but Patrick is harmless. He wanted to know if I had a boyfriend. I said no. He then asked if I could be his girlfriend. It was awkward but funny. I told him that I wouldn't be his girlfriend, but I could be a friend. He accepted that.

Ms. Mosca was working with Fortune on the computer when Fortune flew into a rage. Ms. Mosca put on Kevlar while Ms. Fine and Ms. Goodfellow distracted Fortune. Ms. Mosca then went into action to get Fortune ready for early dismissal. Her mother was going to pick Fortune up at the school instead of waiting for the bus. For a while there, Ms. Mosca took hits and spitting in stride, like it was normal. To be honest, I was a bit scared.

2019-02-22

Today, Fortune's mother met with Ms. Fine in private. They emerged later, and Ms. Fine introduced her to me. Her name is Heather Fallow, but she wants me to call her Heather. She asked Ms. Fine if she could talk privately with me. Ms. Fine said, "Okay."

We went out into the hallway, and Heather asked me, "What was Fortune looking at on the screen with Ms. Mosca yesterday?"

"I don't know. I thought it was counting software," I replied.

"Can you keep an eye on that for me in the future?" she asked. "I'd like to know what's on the computer." She looked at me with trust and hope. "As a favour to me?" She reached out for my hands. "Fortune is a special person. She has a gift. It's only meant for people she likes. She's not fond of Ms. Mosca, unfortunately." She looked at me with intensity. "Can you, please?"

I said, "Sure." She thanked me, and we returned to the classroom in time for dismissal.

This class goes to their buses before the rest of the students are dismissed for the day. The halls get pretty busy and noisy then. I can testify to that through three and a half years of being a student here. It's better that they get out of the school before the rest of the students. Fortune went home with Heather, but as she did, Fortune turned to me and said, "Tile." She then looked away.

Heather confirmed, "Tile." She smiled. "Fortune likes you." She paused. "Keep your eyes open." I remembered her request about watching Fortune's computer screens, so I nodded that I understood. Then they left for the parking lot.

"Tile" made no sense to me. I was glad that Heather and Fortune liked me, but what did "tile" mean? I learned later, after school, what Fortune meant. It was a warning.

For a few weeks now, new plumbing has been installed in the ceiling along the hallway leading to my exit from the school. We walk around the workers and their ladders, separated by that yellow safety tape. An hour after school ended, I was alone. Somehow, above my safe pathway, a ceiling tile fell right in front of me. It almost hit me. It would have hit me if I weren't walking a little more slowly than normal, thinking about the meaning of "tile." Fortune knew ahead of time that that tile was going to fall.

2019-02-25

Ms. Fine completed paperwork for my co-op teacher, Mr. Yacht. While she worked on that, I helped Patrick at the computer. Patrick reached out to hold my hand, and he said, "You're my girlfriend, Tori."

I patted his hand with my free one and withdrew both. "I'm not your girlfriend, Patrick. I'm a co-op student helping here in the classroom."

"Okay," he answered. He turned to Ms. Goodfellow. "Tori is helping, Ms. Goodfellow."

"Yes, she is."

At that moment, Heather entered the classroom with Ms. Edge, the principal, waving from a distance to her daughter. Fortune saw her mother, hesitated, and returned to her work on the computer. A conference ensued in the hall with Ms. Fine, Ms. Edge, and Heather. They called me out to meet with them.

The principal spoke first. "Heather has told me that you and Fortune have developed a friendship of sorts. She likes you."

"Yes. Fortune warned me about something," I said.

"What's that?" Ms. Edge asked.

"About the tile. Fortune said, 'Tile.' I didn't understand at the time. On Friday a tile fell from the ceiling right in front of me as I left the building. Fortune predicted it. I told my mother about it when I arrived at home."

Ms. Edge winced. "Where in the building?" she snapped.

"South-east exit, where they're working on plumbing," I replied.

"Really? You're okay? It didn't hit you?" she added.

"No. I'm fine, thanks. It's nothing, really." I felt a little embarrassed.

"Fortune has the ability to predict things ahead of time," Heather interjected. Ms. Edge and Ms. Fine didn't comment. It seemed they heard that before and looked to each other with silent scepticism. Heather's face flashed disappointment. At least, that was how I interpreted it.

Ms. Edge said, "I'm glad you escaped injury, Tori. Quite fortunate." She smiled. "Come to my office at the end of the period to fill out an accident report with me. I'll speak to the construction supervisor in the meantime." Then she left. Ms. Fine returned to the classroom, leaving Heather and me alone in the hallway.

Heather said, "What's been on the computer screen today, Tori? Anything unusual?"

"I don't think so. We used memory programs for math," I answered. "Can I ask you about that tile falling?"

"It's precognition. Sometimes Fortune is able to see things before the rest of us do. Ms. Fine and Ms. Goodfellow and Ms. Edge don't agree." Heather paused and smiled. "Because they don't believe in Fortune's gift, they can't get the blessing. It doesn't matter for them."

"How did Fortune do that?" I inquired.

Heather leaned closer to me and spoke in a quiet voice. "It's like we're all at the beach, but the waves don't hit the beach squarely; they come in on an angle, hitting one part of the beach first, then breaking along the entire beach. Time is a wave. Fortune experiences the first part of the wave, and then it comes to the rest of us. Time and events often reveal themselves to her first."

I didn't know what to say.

"If your parents are okay with it, Tori, can you come to dinner at our house later this week?"

"I'll ask Mom and Mr. Yacht if it's okay."

"Good. I'll check with you tomorrow. Any night works for us," she responded.

2019-02-26

My mother said it was fine, especially because Fortune prevented an accident from hurting me. She wanted to meet Fortune and her mother too, to say thanks, so I'll propose that to Heather. Then Mom and I talked about next year at university. She told me that she'd be starting next week an additional job in the evening to help me with finances. With both of us working most evenings and weekends, I wonder when we'll see each other.

Mr. Yacht also was pleased that I made personal connections with Fortune and her family. We arranged for two nights from now for me to go to the Fallow house for dinner, right after school.

Fortune was a little cranky today. Something happened on the computer. I was working with Daisy at the time. Ms. Mosca said it was all about some Harry Potter pictures. When I looked at Fortune's screen, a picture of Harry Potter looked normal. I don't know what was so upsetting to Fortune.

2019-02-27

I didn't tell you about Daisy. She prefers not to talk, but she can if she wants. She really likes music and often sings along to what's playing. She especially likes jazz and classical music. Music seems to help her learn basic mathematics. She recites her memorisation of addition in sync with the rhythms of the music. Her favourite song to do that is "Inchworm" by the John Coltrane Quartet. I'm trying to get her to add larger numbers.

Fortune saw me today and predicted an event for me. "Dinner tomorrow night." I laughed. She knew that she was funny.

2019-02-28

I'm getting annoyed with Patrick calling me his girlfriend, but I probably shouldn't. He doesn't know any better. I keep telling him that he's my friend, not my boyfriend. I don't have a boyfriend, and I don't want one. Sometimes it's hard to tell other boys that too.

Daisy can count to one thousand, and she does it out loud. When she's counting, she is focused on that and nothing else. I wonder what she'll do for a living when she leaves high school?

Today I went to the Fallow house for supper. On the outside, it's like all the other houses in the subdivision, but on the inside, it's lovely. They're much richer than we are. Heather met me at the door. Fortune was happy to see me and show me her room. She has her own computer on a very nice office desk. There are posters on the wall of Harry Potter and colour graphs and charts. I thought it was an odd mix of visuals. She has several stuffed animals, but her favourite is a very large, plush, brown bunny with long, floppy ears. Heather prepared chicken breasts stuffed with cheese and broccoli, a salad, and scalloped potatoes. For dessert, we had apple pie. She's a good cook.

I met Fortune's younger brother, Barney. He's twelve. From what I could see, he's a good brother to Fortune.

I met Fortune's father, Peter. He's not a talker. Fortune perhaps gets her quiet nature from him. I asked him what he does. He said he works from home. He didn't elaborate.

Fortune introduced me to each of her stuffed animals by name. I found it odd that she has such affection for them but doesn't bring any to school.

Heather drove me home, and she met my mother. Mom expressed her gratitude for Fortune's warning about the tile. I thanked Heather for the meal and drive home.

2019-03-01

In the classroom, I wished everyone a Happy St. David's Day. Only Ms. Goodfellow understood that.

Ms. Mosca knew about dinner last night with Fortune's family. I asked her how she knew.

"I live across the street from them," she replied.

"Oh, so you know them well," I suggested.

"Not really. They're very secretive." She paused. "Did they tell you how they got all their money?"

"No." I waited.

"They won two lotteries. Now Peter plays stocks with that money."

"They never mentioned it." I figured it wasn't my business.

"It's tough on families when they have children with disabilities. Peter and Heather were in deep debt, beginning a divorce because of Fortune, and then—bingo!—they win twelve million dollars. That changed the direction of their lives. Then—bingo!—they win another eighteen million. Who wins two big lotteries in two years? How did that happen? Well, I'll tell you, Tori: Fortune knows the future." I smiled. "You don't believe me, do you?"

I uttered a small laugh. "You could be right; I don't know. You tell an interesting story, Ms. Mosca."

"She can predict stocks too. I'm sure she helps Peter with that."

"So you and the Fallows are still close friends?"

"Not so much. Before they got rich, we were. Money changes people."

The conservation ended there because Ms. Goodfellow needed me to help Daisy with her Math. Ms. Fine was working alongside Patrick. Ms. Mosca assisted Fortune.

Later, I walked by Ms. Mosca and Fortune at their computer. On the screen, the New York Stock Exchange appeared. Fortune pointed to the screen and said to her, "BANE."

Ms. Mosca responded, "BANE? B-A-N-E? Is that the code for the stock?"

"Yes. Big change is coming. BANE," Fortune replied.

Then Ms. Mosca called Ms. Fine over to help with Fortune. "I'm taking my break now," she told the teacher. That was unusual. Usually breaks are scheduled. Ms. Fine also seemed surprised by this, but she covered for Ms. Mosca, who gathered her purse and pulled out her cell phone as she exited the doorway.

I then returned to Daisy. As she began her counting out loud, Fortune turned to me and said, "Tori." I looked at her. "Six."

Daisy continued her counting. "Seven, eight, nine, ten, eleven, twelve, thirteen, fourteen, fifteen …"

Fortune again said the number with Daisy. "Sixteen." Later, Fortune spoke with her in unison the numbers twenty-two, thirty-one, thirty-eight, forty-five, and forty-nine.

Ms. Fine redirected Fortune's attention away from me to her screen. "Let Daisy work on her own math, and you on yours."

At home, I showed Mom the lottery ticket I bought. She commented, "You're too young to buy this, and besides, we can't afford any wasteful spending." I told her it was my gift to her and that she should check the winning numbers after the draw this evening. She was pleasantly surprised when she did.

2019-03-04

I was away from school with Mom.

2019-03-05

The adults remained silent when I asked about Ms. Mosca's absence today. Later, Patrick told me Ms. Mosca screamed at Fortune in the morning. The principal, Ms. Edge, removed Ms. Mosca from the classroom.

"What did Ms. Mosca say, Patrick?"

"She swore, Tori. That's bad. And she yelled that she lost a lot of money." Then he paused. "Fortune didn't get upset with Ms. Mosca's loudness. That's good."

I need to alter this journal so I can hand it in to Mr. Yacht.

INCLUSION

PRINCIPAL JUDY CARRIOTT required a summary meeting with her more senior vice principal in her office at 4:00 p.m. She had completed her appraisal of Malcolm Reid as required by the Eutopia School Board for vice principals in their first year at a new school assignment.

"I think we see things eye-to-eye, don't we, Malcolm?" she asked.

Appearing somewhat surprised by that question, he responded, "Yes, I suppose we do." His eyes shifted to the wood panelling on the wall behind her desk while she shuffled paper, which he assumed was his appraisal.

"What commended you to me, Malcolm, was that you told me once, before you even arrived here, that you entered education for the sake of students."

"That's true. You have a good memory."

Carriott replied with dry disclosure, "No. I have an exceptional memory."

Malcolm smiled. *And with it an accompanying reputation for vengeance.*

"We have similar outlooks on what a school should do, how it provides learning for students, how it fits into the board's objectives, and how it has good relationships with its community. That's necessary for a common vision of where we are going and the work we do here," Principal Carriott explained. "Your patience with more difficult students is commendable." For emphasis, Carriott lowered her glasses to look over them at Reid. "However, not on this appraisal is the fact that sometimes you have too much patience. Eva Prospect is a prime example." Carriott then cleared her throat, raised her glasses, and returned to examining her evaluation.

"Yes, no doubt," he confirmed. "Eva can be trying, but her behaviour has improved steadily this year." *Judy is firm on discipline.*

"She was enormous trouble before you arrived," Carriott confirmed.

Earlier, I feared Judy's part of that administrative clique in the board. "I'm grateful for your patience with her," Malcolm shared. *They approach student discipline like playing a whack-a-mole game where the highest score wins. But Judy seems to let me do my job.* He paused with his mouth partly open. "It's been a good year here," he added.

"Eutopia East High School has had a good year because you've been an effective vice principal, Malcolm. I appreciate your good relations with staff, parents, and students. You've allowed me to focus on larger issues as I should." She lifted the papers near her chin in an awkward pose, pushed them forward, and held them in front of Malcolm's face. "I want you to read what I have written here on your assessment. And of course, this appraisal will become part of your portfolio for promotion." Some spit from her pronunciation of *portfolio* landed on the evaluation. *She didn't notice. Let it go.*

Malcolm Reid paused. Silence followed. He moved his hands slowly to receive her written appraisal. His eyes made contact with Carriott's expressionless face that transformed into a plastic smile while he drew those papers to himself.

"Go ahead. Read through all of it, but we need to talk about the last paragraph on the third page. If you have questions as you read, please ask them," she directed.

It looks okay. No superlatives, but it's positive, constructive. There's nothing overtly negative here. When Malcolm finished reading her recommendation for promotion, he tilted his head up and asked, "You want me to take more professional development?" He waited

INCLUSION

for her delayed answer. *I get more PD than you do at the board office, and I especially benefit from Principals' Association meetings, which you don't attend. You're the one who doesn't want to leave the building, except when you're told to attend meetings.*

"Well, Malcolm, staying completely current will help you to become a principal."

Malcolm Reid laughed as he asked, "You don't think I'm out of the building too much already?"

Judy Carriott smiled. "Of course not. This is important. Take my advice. Sign up for some conferences. There's one coming up soon on inclusive schools. It looks interesting. Why don't you see if you can still register?"

Upon leaving her office, Malcolm remembered his first year of teaching. His principal at the time evaluated him with a board checklist. All of the boxes had been checked in the Excellent area, except for one item that needed improvement: "Professional Dress." Malcolm looked with disbelief at that principal with his mouth open. Every day Malcolm dressed to the nines. Two-piece and three-piece suits were his teaching uniform. Before teaching, he worked retail in men's clothing. That first principal had grinned and said, "Well, everyone has something to work on." His big hand rested on Malcolm's shoulder. "I'm recommending you for a permanent contract." Malcolm smiled at that memory.

Following Carriott's suggestion, Malcolm attended that conference on inclusive schools. Another vice principal from Eutopia School Board, Lewis Featherstone, chummed along to presentations with him. After each session, they compared notes on their computers. Lewis informed Malcolm of a social gathering later that evening with presenters from the day's meetings. "Come on; let's go. It'll be fun. The Cognitive Continuum sponsors it. Free drinks!"

Just what Lewis needs: free drinks.

Malcolm remembered his conversation with Eva Prospect before he left. "I want you on your absolutely best behaviour until I get back. No trouble, okay? I'm gonna let your mom know that too."

"Don't go. Carriott hates me. Why can't you be principal?" Eva asked.

"Don't give her reason to discipline you. Be good."

Eva Prospect paused and then replied, "Hey, Mr. Reid. Don't worry. I'll be like an angel." She reviewed her previous indiscretions. "I won't swear at teachers or vice principals or principals. At least in public. And I won't punch anyone. No fights, no vandalism, no stealing, nothing."

I sure hope that Eva's staying off the radar and people aren't pushing her buttons.

As Malcolm Reid and Lewis Featherstone approached the hospitality suite along a cavernous hallway, party noise amplified exponentially. In the room, laughter and dialogue with some background music banished peace. Alcohol seemed to be everyone's best companion. To hear dialogue, conversations required volume.

While Lewis made a beeline to the drinks area, Malcolm observed. Many conversations engaged their participants. A large television broadcast a basketball game, but only two men stood watching it. A smaller room attached to the larger one formed the bottom part of a large letter *L*. People there looked less engaged. They sat in sofas and armchairs. *Where do all these people come from?* Closer to the drinks area, several chic women conversed with handsome, equally dapper males. *Young, upwardly mobile, and already higher up, I believe.* He smiled at people as they brushed by him in this crowded room. Several presenters scattered throughout the room in discussion with people from the in crowd.

Lewis handed Malcolm a beer and shouted, "I'm not sure that we belong here." Malcolm nodded in agreement.

As they travelled the room, Lewis and Malcolm made banter with whoever looked disconnected from conversation, much like bees pollinating several different flowers. The purpose of each conversation was to make personal connections. It was not networking. Neither Eutopia District high school vice principal cared or saw it necessary to do that for his professional career. Lewis and Malcolm enjoyed people. The conversations rarely had anything to do with education. After Lewis's third beer, Malcolm thought it wise to sit Lewis down in couches in the bottom, quieter part of the L-shaped room.

In a chair opposite them sat alone a young, tall, professionally attired black woman. She looked familiar. "Hi, I'm Lewis. This is Malcolm." Both men stood to shake her hand, and then they sat back down.

"Hi, I'm Tanya."

We saw her speak. Duh! Malcolm asked for verification. "You're Tanya Edwards?" However, he didn't wait for her confirmation. "Lewis and I enjoyed your session on inclusive education and social justice."

"Thank you. Where are you from, gentlemen?"

Lewis waved his beer bottle around as he spoke with his hands. "We're nearby, kinda local, from the Eutopia School Division. I'm Lewis Featherstone at Eutopia South High School, and Malcolm Reid is at Eutopia East High School."

"What do you teach?" she asked.

"We don't teach any more. We're vice principals," Lewis explained. "On principle, we're in charge of vice."

Tanya Edwards smiled. "And what's your favourite vice, Lewis?"

"You're looking at it: beer." Lewis looked to Malcolm and then placed his hand on Malcolm's knee. "Get me another beer, would you, buddy? This one's screaming for companionship."

Malcolm checked to see how self-aware Lewis was. "Another? Are you sure?"

"We're not driving anywhere tonight, Malcolm. Relax. I like to be in the loop. Or be looped. Actually, both." He looked at Tanya and laughed.

Malcolm stood. "Would you like anything, Tanya?"

"No, I'm still nursing a water. Thanks, Malcolm."

Malcolm ventured toward the drinks area. *If there's truth in wine, for Lewis there's butt-naked honesty in beer. Why am I doing this?* He looked around the room again and noticed Tanya's colleagues grouping together. While he walked by them with Lewis's beer, he overheard their conversation about disappearing to a club nearby. "What about Tanya?" one asked. The man to whom the question was addressed simply shook his head no.

After winding his way back to Tanya and Lewis, Malcolm Reid glanced back at the group. It was disbanding and heading for the main exit. He handed Lewis the beer and sat down. Lewis expressed excitement. "Thanks, Malcolm. Tanya here was telling me about how she got on the circuit. It's fascinating."

"I was telling Lewis that I'm only a junior member of the speaking circuit. We're in Denver next week, Chicago the week after, and Vancouver after that."

Lewis enthusiastically relayed, "The company she works for, the Cognitive Continuum, promotes her books."

Without hesitation Malcolm asked, "I'm curious, and I hope you don't mind me asking, but what's the corporate cut? And do you get what the other speakers here earn to speak and to sell books?"

An awkward pause followed. "It's a forthright question, Malcolm."

"Of course. A small amount of fast-acting alcohol on an empty stomach may have contributed to that, but my natural curiosity about what people earn and how systems work overrode my sense of propriety. I'm sorry." Malcolm visited his beer for a brief moment. "However, I noticed that your peers left this party without you."

Tanya inquired, "What are you saying?"

Lewis interjected, "Malcolm is saying that maybe you need some alcohol too."

Tanya laughed. "As a new, junior partner, I'm compensated fairly. I have to earn my way into a senior partnership. I'm working hard on it." She stood. "Gentlemen, I need to go now. It's been good talking with you." When she examined the larger part of the room, she stopped and observed that her colleagues were no longer in the room. A glimpse of sadness preceded a subtle twinge of pain on her face when her back briefly bowed. It was if a wasp had stung her in the back. Then she relaxed, and her discomfort vanished.

Leaping to his feet, Lewis with beer bottle in hand grabbed both her arms and gently guided her back to her seat. "You're not leaving. We're kidnapping you, and we're forcing you to drink wine with us. Red or white? I'm assuming you're a wine drinker." Tanya Edwards's thought process became transparent. The Clash's "Should I Stay or Should I Go" came to Malcolm's mind as he observed her. She chose to sit down. Lewis started to bolt but returned, handed his beer to Malcolm, and sped away.

"When he drinks, it's hard to slow him down," Malcolm Reid advised. "It's good that he comes here to reacquaint himself with why he's such a good VP. He's in it for the kids, even in a tough school."

"So what do you hope to get out of the conference, Malcolm?" Tanya asked.

Vice Principal Reid didn't want to tell her the truth: *I've come here to be promoted. That's insulting to her and the people here.* Then he abandoned caution and laughed when he said, "A promotion."

Tanya Edwards chortled. "Me too!"

At that moment, Lewis returned with one glass of white wine and one glass of red wine. He placed them uncomfortably close to her face. "Which one?" Tanya, like a graceful dancer, moved her hand and arm to choose the red. That smooth motion continued to her sipping from the glass. Lewis turned to Malcolm and handed him the glass of white. "Don't say that I don't think of you."

After a couple more drinks, Tanya further explored Malcolm's comment. "So if you come here, you get promoted?"

"It's not that simple. I was advised that if I want to become a principal, I must attend more professional development," Malcolm answered.

"That's bullshit!" interjected Lewis. "You're pretty professionally developed with all that stuff you do for the Principals' Association. You know more than your bosses do. They should learn from you.

The problem with you is that you intimidate senior management. That's why you've not been promoted: they're scared of you."

Discomfort with Lewis's comments displayed on Malcolm's face. He swallowed a large gulp of wine. *I hope he's wrong, but Lewis Featherstone knows more about Eutopia's politics than I do. He's been turned down five times for promotion, and it isn't because he's bad at the job. He's good. He's there for kids first and foremost. I'd want him as my principal. But his bitterness about the system can't overtake me. I have to stay positive.* "Even if you're right, Lewis, I have to take the advice of people who tell me I'm worthy of the responsibility."

Tanya appeared uncomfortable. She looked out at the room that had largely emptied. "Excuse me, gentlemen. I'll be right back." She stood and walked away.

Both men looked at her as she left without announcement. "Maybe it's a bathroom thing," Lewis guessed.

Malcolm mused. "I hope we haven't dominated the conversation."

"No, she would have said goodbye." Lewis drank from his beer bottle. "We should get something to eat."

Malcolm ignored that suggestion. He wanted to finish another train of thought from earlier. "You know, Judy Carriott has written some nice things about me," he said.

"She said nice things about me too, but it never amounted to anything. She's not about the students. She's about her reputation in the Eutopia board."

"The Eutopia board is our employer. We both signed a contract with the board. We have an obligation of loyalty to it," Malcolm emphasised.

Lewis reacted, "Bullshit! Where does that come from?"

"The lawyers at the Principals' Association." Malcolm smiled. "See? I pay attention at those meetings. I even take notes and pass them along to you and other administrators." Malcolm leaned forward in a mocking manner. "You read those notes, don't you, Lewis?"

Lewis's hand gestures caused his drink to spill. "It's about kingdoms, Malcolm. Every senior manager in the Eutopia board has a kingdom. They demand deference and loyalty and servitude. Self-interest runs education. The teachers' union is about the union, and the board is about the board. The Principals' Association is about the Principals' Association. The fact that students graduate with a diploma is a hopeful wish and a fortunate by-product of what we do. It's rarely about the kids. Look at board committees. There are ones on parental involvement, safe schools, technology applications, labour relations, community outreach, best practices, anti-bullying, and inclusive education."

"Lewis, some of those initiatives have made a difference in students' lives."

"Don't get me wrong—they're all important and do affect the lives of students. But they seem more like busy work or lip service to problems. You and I know that some of the biggest bullies going belong to senior management. Maybe these schemes and committees might solve or even prevent troubles, but they don't change many things for students. Good intentions can't change students with lousy lives. Most students will be successful despite the crap that's thrown at them. And despite the rhetoric about student success initiatives, education doesn't care about unsuccessful students, nor does society as a whole. They get to flip burgers, live on welfare, live on the street, or go to jail. They don't get past Go; they don't collect two hundred dollars!"

Extending Lewis's comments, Malcolm pondered Eva Prospect. *She's worth saving. It's been worthwhile. I think she's going to make it.*

Tanya Edwards reappeared, holding a tray loaded with water bottles, pizza, and a bottle of wine. "Empty stomachs need food and hydration." Lewis and Malcolm expressed their gratitude, and Tanya continued. "I hear passion in your voice, Lewis, even from a distance. Did I miss the best part?"

Malcolm responded, "How intuitive of you, Tanya. Thank you. Does that mean you want to stay and listen to rants?"

"May I rant too?" she asked.

"Sure, misery loves company," Lewis slurred. After Tanya placed the tray on a coffee table beside the couch, Lewis claimed a water bottle.

Malcolm invited, "Tell us what makes you angry."

"Angry? That's personal. Gentlemen, I hardly know you."

Lewis wryly smiled at Tanya. "Tell me who said this: 'I am protective of my own personal life, but I must confess that I enjoy watching people that don't mind telling it all.'"

Appearing puzzled, Tanya replied, "I don't know. Probably not Plato."

"Partial points for that answer. It was Tyra Banks."

"Really? Tyra Banks?" Tanya gathered a slice of pizza, napkins, and a glass of wine. "Why do you know that, Lewis?"

"I pay attention to beautiful women with intelligence."

"Are you flirting with me, Lewis?"

"Yes."

Tanya laughed at his honesty. "Okay. I suppose I can let my guard down a bit." She gulped wine. "Angry?" That's not the right word. It limits how I feel from moment to moment. I also feel hurt, disappointment, sadness, injustice, doubt, pessimism, and hopelessness, but right now I feel none of that. Leftover pizza, wine, and real people for company take my blues away." With her hands full, she celebrated with a restrained booty shake before she sat down. "Woo!"

"So what got you into speaking tours?" Malcolm inquired.

"Teaching, then research, then publication, then public speaking, then the Learning Continuum offers this black woman a junior partnership. I've been with the company for almost two years. The partners want me to boost my profile more."

"They want you to boost your profile. Why don't they boost your profile?" asked Lewis.

"It shouldn't be theirs or my responsibility. Doing publicity together would seem right," she answered. "I'm still researching, and I'm ready to publish again, but they're not helpful with those things.

They have their stars, and I'm not one of them. Not that I want to be a star. I want to make a difference in students' experiences in schools."

Lewis inserted with triumphant righteousness, "You see? You're about the students. They're about the corporation. You're on the bottom. You're their token …"

Tanya cut Lewis short with her interruption and signal to not speak. "Oh, I know. That's not going to stop or limit me. Believe me. They don't know the force they're dealing with." She reached for more wine. She topped up her glass, said, "Cheers," clicked glasses with Lewis and Malcolm, took a sip, and then reached for a piece of pizza.

After he checked his phone for messages from the school and saw none, a troubling notion popped into Malcolm's consciousness. *Plenty of board emails, but why are there no school messages?* He considered this for a moment.

Lewis addressed Malcolm's vacant mien. "Hey, Malcolm, where are you?"

"It's just a thing from work."

Lewis scolded him. "Stop that. Enjoy your time away from the office. Really. And turn off your phone. The Eutopia board doesn't own you."

Judy told me the same thing, "Turn off your phone," on Thursday. "You're right. Sorry." He shut down his cell phone. Malcolm rejoined the conversation. After a few minutes, the trio chose to venture out to various nightlife hangouts. True to Lewis's advice, Malcolm delighted in his evening without thoughts about work.

The inclusive schools conference ended Saturday at noon. He returned to work Monday morning to a flashing red light on his office phone. Eva Prospect's mother left two messages on Friday. *I was only gone one day!* The first shouted with emotion and pain; the second appealed for intervention. Principal Judy Carriott threw Eva out of Eutopia East High School. He waited for his computer to boot.

At that moment Judy Carriott materialised in his office. Without preamble she rationalised for Malcolm, "Eva and her mother were obnoxious again, Malcolm. It was the worst I've ever seen it, and it was the last straw. With the support of our superintendent, I've arranged for her to attend Eutopia Central High School. We get one of their headaches, and they get one of ours. The change of scenery will be good for Eva. The good news for you is that the new student is not your responsibility."

Malcolm Reid regarded Judy Carriott with sadness, disappointment, and new insight. "At least I should call her mother. She left me two messages." He reached for the phone.

"She knows what's been decided. She wants you to reverse things, no doubt, but from the board's perspective it's all done."

"I realise that. I just thought I should call her out of respect for her and Eva."

"Malcolm, don't call." Carriott's tone and glare indicated a line Malcolm should not cross. "Remember, team players get promotions."

THE LONELY BEAT ON SIMCOE STREET

THE FAKE-LEATHER COWBOY makes Port Perry's streets safe, walking the Simcoe Street beat with a police radio in hand, wearing a black hat so that the bad guys do not see him coming. He does not strike fear into their hearts, and he is as gentle as an Amish Mennonite. His diligence keeps him thin, and citizens give him respect by giving him space and silence.

He is a lonely man, looking for life's meaning. It passed him by some time ago. The black-hatted, fake-leather cowboy is horseless and alone. When the sun sets, he is freed to range home to his daughter and her family. There, she has a cold meal waiting for him. She points to it at the end of the counter. His grandchildren do not acknowledge him, but his granddaughter's cat rubs firmly against his legs, silently and loyally welcoming him home.

He chooses not to warm the meal in the microwave oven, and in so doing, he also does not face the wrath of his daughter for his tardiness—and because the only technology he masters is his police radio.

Forlorn at the kitchen table, he ponders his existence silently during each slow, thorough, and exaggerated bite. He takes the dirty utensils and empty plate to the sink to wash them by hand without dish soap. He places them in the drying rack and retreats to his room in the far corner of the basement. There, he listens to the police band in preparation for the next day.

His mission is misunderstood. As the prophet is not esteemed in his hometown, so also is the fake-leather cowboy. When a few disrespectful teenagers say he is insane, he pulls a neatly folded paper from his jacket. "I'm not crazy. See? The doctors signed it." He displays with pride and authority the official document that confirms his assertion. "Where are your papers to show you're sane?" he then asks them. He folds his paper with care and returns it to his pocket. They look at him sideways and scoff, insulting him as he spritely continues on his mission to secure Simcoe Street.

Because he patrols, there is little crime. Once he is witness to a traffic accident on Simcoe Street, and he is diligent in describing the incident to the investigating officer from a safe verbal distance so he does not interfere with the police probe. His explanation is done one sentence at a time with punctuated pauses. His body leans forward to accentuate each sentence. A second officer arrives, and she shoos him away.

With every hero, there is a history. The fake-leather cowboy is an enigma, but with careful study, he can be exposed. He is a man whose past formed him into the legend he is today. He wears the scars of mental illness, but his youthful gait and skin reveal a man of internal anguish only. What that might have been is unclear to most, but others know, and they guard the secret for fear of dishonouring their professions.

On North Simcoe Street, there are two seniors' homes. It is not customary for Alzheimer's patients to wander from the homes, but on one January day it is true. Mrs. Heard somehow has managed to escape two hundred metres south of the home in her nightgown. On his rounds, the fake-leather cowboy (also wearing earmuffs under his flat-top cowboy hat because it is considerably colder than freezing) finds Mrs. Heard talking kindly to him. She promises to speak to her former neighbour about the bourgeoning grub problem on their adjoining lawns. The hero and Mrs. Heard are two kindred spirits, and he wraps his fake-leather coat and his arms around her. She is grateful, and the fake-leather cowboy discerningly returns her to the correct seniors' home from which she escaped. The desk clerk is surprised that Mrs. Heard would leave the home on such a cold day with so few clothes.

He does not seek glory. Yet his reputation has grown because the traffic along Simcoe Street includes significant out-of-town commuters. They spot him as they drive, and they wonder who he is. Simcoe Street runs north and south throughout the whole town, but it originates at Lake Ontario in the city of Oshawa, some thirty-five kilometres south of Port Perry, and it continues equidistantly north to its completion at the Glenarm Road. It is an important route for transportation to the urban south from northern rural areas and from the city to cottage country. All traffic flows through Port Perry, home of the fake-leather cowboy. His heroics have not gone unnoticed in what was once Ontario County.

He remembers that municipality, and the change by the provincial government that happened thirty-seven years ago—the one that joined most of Durham County with most of Ontario County—confuses him. It is renamed Durham Region, so the history that defines his youth is gone. He cannot change the past, and he cannot lament its loss. The shock treatments and drug therapies have ensured that.

The capital town of the old Ontario County is Whitby. To get there, one takes Highway 12, which runs parallel to Simcoe Street, three kilometres west. As a small town and now an expansive city, it has hosted a reputable mental health hospital for the province of Ontario for many years. The fake-leather cowboy occasionally returns to Whitby, driven there by his daughter to speak as an outpatient with his social worker. These appointments are rarely convenient for his daughter, a shift-working custodian at North Eutopia Junior and Senior High School.

He does not enjoy visiting there even though it is a much more hospitable, modern facility now. The worker asks caring questions, and when he visits, he is asked to wait outside the social worker's office while his daughter speaks privately to the worker. Daily she thinks to herself that her father came through all of that chemical and electrical experimentation as well as can be expected—and that it has been good for him.

Occasionally commuters find the fake-leather cowboy darting in front of cars on Simcoe Street. They slam their brakes to avoid hitting the man with their vehicles. Unfortunately, he has been nudged twice by cars, but no damage has been done except to the nerves of the drivers. Being a hero sometimes demands sacrifice from others.

Intermittently, he is approached by visitors to Port Perry for directions. He is a kind, patient ambassador when they ask. As a long-time resident of Ontario County, the hero provides accurate and thorough directions to the lost and guideless. As a matter of course, this annoys some impatient motorists who follow the visitors. They, in turn, attempt to pass the queue and the lost, causing potential mishaps. However, when his lengthy illuminations are complete, the lost soon find their way to their destinations with a clear sense of route.

Tonight, the fake-leather cowboy listens casually to the police radio band while re-reading for the ninety-seventh time out loud a book on insects. At times without awareness of his daughter as an audience, he involuntarily recites paragraphs from the book. However, this evening he reads it with a fresh view and without an audience, enjoying the resonance of his own voice, absorbing its meaning as if he is reading it for the first time. Somehow his heroic mind permits him to keep his cadence opposite the cacophonic interference of the radio. He also unconsciously caresses his granddaughter's cat that has wedged its head and then its body through the nearly closed door and has unguardedly and affectionately placed itself on his lap.

It is a late August Tuesday evening. The sun has set, and the remnant of light in the western sky shows a deep purple with a faint hint of orange around three small adjoined cumulus clouds. In the peaceful picture of the day's fading, there suddenly is an urgent call for police assistance with a fire on Old Simcoe Road and Chimney

Hill Drive. The fake-leather cowboy must make a difficult decision. Although he lives four short blocks away from the fire's location, Old Simcoe Road is not his beat.

It is a perplexing area to him. It is the edge of a new subdivision. Yet on the corner next to the new are the old and faithful buildings: the curling rink, the Legion Hall, and a century-old home with an old barn. For the sake of reminiscence and the hope for heroism, the fake-leather cowboy re-establishes his uniform. He scurries out the front door as his daughter asks for an explanation. She does not receive one. Oddly, in dog-like fidelity, the cat bolts through the front door with him to follow him.

When he arrives at the corner, there are fire trucks, police cruisers, and curious onlookers. Flashing lights add to the excitement and chaos of the scene. He sees flames rising high above the barn, that sagging, lilting landmark that contrasts the new homes west and north-west of it. Without betraying his heroic stoicism by audibly weeping, his eyes are given reluctant permission to release tears. Memories course to consciousness because this barn, the old home, and the farm that is now a subdivision are his childhood home.

While blocking the roads and redirecting traffic, constables are also attempting to move the crowd well back for safety's sake. Employing his characteristic inconspicuousness, overlooked by the authorities and crowd, the fake-leather cowboy relocates into the subdivision. He strategically walks between two houses that back onto the burning barn property. The closest firefighters are not yet on the west side of the barn. They are busy yelling instructions to each other, and they do not notice his awkward launch over the chain-link fence. He moves closer to the fire slowly, deliberately.

Before the fire, the photogenic barn has not been in use because its precarious structure prevents safe entry. As he nears it, he believes he hears the sound of a cat mewing for help. At this moment, he begins staccato movements to find the source of the cry for help, but this betrays his discretion. It is then that he becomes visible to a firefighter, who yells at him, attracting the attention of others.

A police officer yells and waves, "Buddy, get back from the fire!"

He freezes into tableau for about ten seconds with a pained, conflicted facial expression and a body position that shows him going in two directions.

"Buddy, get out of there!"

He remains silent, but his repeated movement toward and away from the fire in short steps comically reminds the disengaged onlooker of Charlie Chaplin's tramp—except he wears a black, fake-leather coat and a black, flat-top cowboy hat.

As our hero is short-circuiting, the officer rushes in to tackle him. It is a struggle, but the officer is able to pull him away from the fire. Another officer and a citizen come to the first officer's assistance.

"The cat!"

"What cat?"

He points to the fire. "The cat!"

All four men are now under the spotlight from a police cruiser. It highlights the smoke and the shrinking flames behind them. Also visible are water drops from the firefighters' hoses that indiscriminately and graciously fall on them.

The first officer assures him. "Buddy, cats are too smart to get stuck in that."

"No, I heard one!"

"Come on. I'll take you home."

He protests weakly to the officer, "I am home," and he rises slowly, painfully. He begins the slow journey to the police car with his head low. Others examine him with curiosity.

The firefighters move closer to the scorched barn, and a lightness to their approach begins as the fire fades. Among them, jovial, good-natured kidding begins. The crowd thins.

The hero remains in the back of the cruiser, staring at the barn, the only barn left from the farm that he knows was his home as a boy. The old farmhouse, once elegant in its time, remains in faded keep. The other barns have gone, and the land from the farm has sprouted a subdivision. The cowboy sees beyond the present reality to a different time, one where he belongs, where a vast field of corn, several barns, and old tractors rest. He sees his mother hanging clothes on the clothesline. His younger sister is playing on a swing under a maple tree. His father is fixing one of the tractors. His older brother assists. He is petting a kitty near the barn that still exists, and that charred, scarred remnant brings him out of his pleasurably nostalgic journey and into the present.

After he has been escorted home, he endures the scolding from his daughter. In bed, he cannot sleep. His thoughts constantly return to the safety of cats. Thoughts are one thing; actions are another.

Next morning, after ducking under the yellow caution tape, two fire inspectors approach the fire scene on Old Simcoe Road. They are cautious as they enter the south side of the small barn where a gaping hole in the wall and randomly piled timbers from the roof have fallen. A cat approaches them from the top of the pile, rubbing their legs affectionately and mewing. The larger man reaches down to pet the cat, and after initial contact, the cat moves back to the edge of the pile, rubbing against a black cowboy boot affixed to what appears to be a leg.

Without much dialogue, the two men begin to move the wood. They find an old man wearing black jeans with a black, fake-leather coat, black cowboy boots, and nearby, a black flat-top cowboy hat. There is a sizeable pool of blood near his head, mixed in with the grey water from the fire, not fully coagulated and still bright red. There is no pulse. The cat licks the fake-leather cowboy's wound at the head, perhaps knowing the worst, perhaps honouring him.

The beat on Simcoe Street needs a new hero.

DRAMATIC IRONY

WHEN MARCIA JOHNSON has decisions to make, she consults with her mentor and friend at Eutopia West Community High School, Rocky Goodchild, who teaches English. They go out for meals together between school days and school evening events such as parent-teacher interviews. Today, she seeks his opinion in the English department office at a small, round, grey table with two institutionally blue chairs by it while she opens a chocolate bar. Marcia announces to Rocky, "I've narrowed it down to three plays that I'm sure would interest students and audiences alike. But I think my preference is a play by Norma Champlain."

"Good. Which play?"

"*Post Meridiem at Virginia Beach*," she says, looking for approval from Rocky.

Rocky Goodchild immediately connects to the Internet to research. "The *New York Times* gave it a so-so review in 1962, but, others liked it. I know the play. It's fun. The kids should do it. Norma Champlain is a well-known name, so your audience will attend for that reason too. And it's safe." Goodchild pauses for effect. "The zealots can't complain."

Marcia marvels that Rocky has no fear of the zealots, but he knows how to avoid conflict. He also is a larger-than-life character, and his

DRAMATIC IRONY

intelligence is intimidating. Zealots cannot match his influence and charm. They leave him alone. In fact, he intimidates most people. Conversely, Marcia bristles when conflict happens. She apprehends the zealots because they can make things difficult, something she has experienced before at Eutopia West.

"How do you get away with it, Rocky? Why don't the zealots go after you?" she asks. "Why do they come after me?"

"Because they think I'm crazy, and they think you're normal. They think I'm evil, but that you're good—not perfect, but good." Rocky points his long index finger at Marcia in warning. "Your niceness makes them want doctrinal purity from you. They want to make you perfect like them. They want to control you. For the zealots, I'm a lost cause," Rocky replies with a superior grin. "You know that I wrote erotica. Novels. They did quite well."

Marcia's eyes widen. She looks through his black-framed glasses to catch a hint of untruthfulness, perhaps exaggeration, perhaps shock value. "What?" She observes his widening smile. "Is that public knowledge?"

"No. God, no." Rocky watches Marcia eat her chocolate. "I wrote erotica for a while after my first divorce. It made me money. I needed money. Betty cleaned me out, so I needed an alternative source of income, one that I could hide. I used a pen name. I still receive royalties for them. Are you going to eat all that chocolate?"

Suddenly, Marcia thinks about the significance of her mindless activity. *Weight. Watching weight. Don't finish this.* "Here, Rocky. Finish this." Marcia slides the remaining chocolate in its wrapper across the table.

"Thanks, Marcia. You know, next to women, I love chocolate best."

With that decision finalised, Ms. Johnson announces to her second semester grade 12 dramatic arts class at Eutopia West, "Anna, I want you to be the student director of the play I've chosen." Students congratulate Anna, and then Ms. Johnson resumes. "I will do the casting to save you from having to make those choices among your friends. In fact, we will have double casting, so that we involve as many students as possible, and we have insurance if someone is sick during our performance time. We don't have understudies. All actors will perform twice. Those not performing will of course be involved in the production end of things." The other students seem to understand and accept her logic. Anna's love of theatre makes her a reasoned choice.

With casting decisions complete, work on *Post Meridiem at Virginia Beach* follows a schedule with expectation that lines are memorised when classes return after Easter break. Some of the students plan to escape in Hawaii. Marcia's break includes marking papers, visits with family, and if weather permits, some skiing.

Her return on Monday morning after Easter vacation requires crutches. Her principal, Alvin T. Umberside, whom she admires and whose support she greatly appreciates, greets her at the door, assisting her entrance. "What happened?" he asks.

"Oh, a little knee twist on the ski hill," Marcia replies. Alvin notes no cast on her leg. "Doctor says to take it easy on it for a week."

"I'm glad it's not too serious. Before you go to your office, could we meet in my office first?" She looks at his face to read him. He continues, "Let me help you with that backpack."

Marcia inquires, "Everything okay, Alvin?"

"Let's talk in my office." She silently accompanies him to his office, and he shuts the door behind her when she enters.

What kind of caca am I in right now? Marcia sits in the brown leather chair in front of Umberside's desk. He sits on a larger brown leather chair on the other side. *This chair doesn't feel as comfortable as other times I've been here.* "So what's up, Alvin?"

"Marcia, I've had a complaint, so I wanted to make you aware of it. It's about the play you've chosen."

A complaint. First thing after the break. What? "Did you get this complaint this morning?"

"No, last night. It was relayed to me by the superintendent," Alvin answers. "The chair of the board sent it to him, and our local trustee passed it along before that."

"Who registered the complaint? Or perhaps a better question should be, Who doesn't know about it beside me?"

"You know Mrs. Paddock ..."

"Yes, Lilly Paddock. Her daughter's in my grade 12 class. Monica."

"A fine family, well respected ..."

Marcia winces. "Alvin, you know how much political clout she has."

"I think our meeting this morning proves it," Umberside responds while his elbows rest on the desk, and he wrings his hands. "Look, Marcia, I don't want to tell you what to do, but could I request that you meet with Mrs. Paddock and work this out with her at her house?"

"Her house? Alvin, shouldn't it be here at the school, or at least some place neutral? You're not going to be there to support me?"

"No, Marcia. I think you can do this on your own. You're quite capable ... at her home."

Marcia Johnson stares at her leader, whom she respects. *Are you more scared of Lilly Paddock than I am? I think you are. You're placing trust in me. You think I can solve this so you don't have to. I guess that's another kind of support. Or not.*

"Sure, I'll meet with her. I don't understand what's so racy about a Norma Champlain play. She's a critically acclaimed and appreciated writer. The play is pretty safe territory. That's partly why I chose it."

Alvin T. Umberside looks at her with what she interprets as sincerity. "I agree it's harmless. You can fix this. I have faith in you," he proclaims.

Marcia reclaims her crutches and stands. "Thanks for letting me know, Alvin." He helps her with her backpack. She stops at the door and turns around. "I'll fix it. I won't like it, but I'll do it."

At the end of the school day, Ms. Johnson pulls her coat from the coat rack in the English office. Rocky grins at her as she prepares to leave. "Have fun with Mrs. Paddock." Marcia thinks twice about swearing at him. Then he erupts into laughter from a snicker. *Asshole.*

"Fine friend you are," she ejects.

"You forgot something."

"What?"

"Your cross. Mrs. Paddock wants to nail you to it." Rocky laughs again during her exit.

This is her first time seeing the Paddock home. It's an impressively large, modern house on the river. Before she can ring the doorbell, Lilly Paddock swings the wide front door open to reveal herself and her affluent home. "Welcome to the Paddock family home, Marcia."

"Thank you, Lilly."

With reference to Marcia's crutches, Lilly asks, "What happened to you?" Light conversation continues as she sits on a chair at the sizable dining room table. Lilly offers a glass of water, which Marcia accepts.

"The children are all off at their after-school activities. No one else is here to interfere with our conversation," Lilly assures Marcia.

Their conversation is civil and respectful. Lilly Paddock is a fan of Norma Champlain's writing. Having read *Post Meridiem at Virginia Beach,* her problems with this play are smoking onstage, characters changing behind towels, and bikinis.

"I'm sure you realise, Lilly, that bikinis are central to unravelling the story and catching criminals. It's during the time of introduction of bikini fashion, and believe me, they're not the revealing ones that some young women wear today. In the play, the character in the bikini helps to solve the crime. She's an undercover cop," Marcia argues. "She's the distraction that unmasks the thieves."

"Yes, I get all that. It's just that your double casting is wrong. I don't mind the skinny girl wearing the bikini, but not the other one."

What? "You mean, Rita." Lilly Paddock nods acknowledgement with disgust. Suddenly, a Beatles song plays in Marcia's head: "Lovely Rita."

As planned, Marcia meets Rocky at Loose Goose Pub. "So you worked out a deal with Lilly Paddock. Good for you. Alvin T. Umberside will be happy. So will everyone else up the chain of command. Now, let me buy you that drink that I promised. What'll it be?"

"I don't know. What are you drinking?" Marcia asks.

"Glenfiddich."

"Then that's what I'll have too," she responds.

"An ambrosial drink. Next to women, I love Glenfiddich best," Rocky replies. "So what did you give up?"

"No changes on casting or bikinis. But no smoking on stage, and no changing behind towels." *I can't tell the royalty company, but they aren't sending anyone from New York to see the play.*

"You did well, kid. Casting? What was that about?" Rocky probes.

"She was fine with the skinny girl in a bikini, but not happy about the other girl." Rocky asks who the actors are for the role, and Marcia supplies names.

"Neither girl, or should I say woman, lacks endowment in feminine beauty," Rocky contributed with diplomacy. "My god, Marcia. If they aren't eighteen yet, then they're close. They graduate in two months. Here's what I see. Lilly's daughter must behave like an angel, but she allows her son to be a little hellion. There's bit of a double standard for all the zealots, actually, when I reflect on it.

There's one standard for boys and another for girls. What's Lilly Paddock's problem?" He sips more. "The not-skinny one, Rita, does have considerably more real estate though." He pauses. "Up top."

"That's for sure," Marcia confirms. Goodchild and Johnson raise their glasses, clink them, and take a sip. "Bottoms up," she says.

Later, Rocky stands to leave. "Good night, Marcia. Have a good sleep. Eat something. You look as though you lost weight."

"Probably stress. That's not how I want to trim down."

"And now I'm off to see my lovely wife, my third and favourite wife." He looks at his wristwatch. "She should be home from work now. I adore Jeannie, you know. We are absolutely enraptured with each other."

"Yes, I know," Marcia confirms with a smile.

"I'm firmly committed to the institution of marriage now, Marcia."

When you taught me, you were on your first marriage, to Betty. The second wife, Shawna, was a rebound thing. Besides, she was too young for you. "I'm glad you've found happiness, Rocky. But after two divorces and three marriages, you'd better be committed."

Rocky crosses his eyes and rolls them. His body shakes. "Commit me, please! Someone, please commit me!" Marcia laughs. Rocky leaves.

The next day, without going into any details why, Marcia Johnson explains to her student director, Anna, what must change. She accepts this alteration without any questions, but she does look at her teacher with a knowing look that says, *There's something wrong here, but I don't want to make things worse, so I won't say anything.* Marcia chooses to ignore it and move onward.

DRAMATIC IRONY

Near the end of semester and graduation, *Post Meridiem at Virginia Beach* plays for four nights to sell-out crowds appreciative of talents exhibited by these young thespians.

Rocky and his third wife, Jeannie, meet with Marcia Johnson at Loose Goose Pub after the fourth performance for a late snack. "How was the cast party?" Jeannie inquires.

"I was so proud of those guys. I had to let them know, so I put in a brief appearance and made a short congratulatory speech, but I'm glad Anna's parents are supervising. I don't want the responsibility," Marcia replies. Marcia, Rocky, and Jeannie talk about the play after ordering pizza.

"I saw you talking with that vacuous woman after the show," Rocky observes. "After that theatrical triumph, I hope you rubbed Lilly Paddock's nose in the make-up kits."

"That wouldn't have been a very gracious thing to do," Marcia retorts.

Rocky laughs and jests, "But you thought about it, didn't you?" Marcia smiles, but she remains silent. "You're right: those kids did a great job. Couldn't see what all the fanatical fuss was all about. Those kids played their parts with commitment. What a triumph." Rocky pauses. "Excellent show. You know, ladies, next to women, I love theatre best."

Marcia turns to Jeannie to address her. "Rocky's love for theatre is contagious, Jeannie. He passed it on to me when I was his student." Jeannie smiles and rubs Rocky's arm.

"You were a very committed student, Marcia. You've carried that dedication with you into the teaching profession. That's why I insisted that Alvin T. Umberside hire you."

When the pizza comes, Rocky Goodchild declares that, next to women, he loves pizza best.

After graduation ceremony, Anna leaves friends and family to find her dramatic arts teacher. She is talking to Mr. Umberside. Others wait to speak to him, so Anna seizes her opportunity and pulls Ms. Johnson away to speak privately. Umberside and Johnson signal to each other that they continue their conversation later.

In their tête-à-tête, Anna and Marcia Johnson share their appreciation for each other. The teacher congratulates Anna's accomplishment as a high school graduate, but Anna demonstrates a need to inform her teacher of something. She looks around to ascertain if others are listening.

"What is it, Anna?"

"I want you to know something about the play. The problem you had with Mrs. Paddock wasn't bikinis."

Marcia cannot contain her astonishment. "How did you know about that? I never told you."

"During the Easter break, when students went to Hawaii, a few of them turned eighteen, including Rita—especially Rita," Anna explains. "She celebrated."

"Did she get drunk?"

"No. It's more than that. A lot more. It was on display for a few days. She damaged her reputation beyond repair. I don't want to go into details. It wasn't bikinis. It was her." Anna looks at her teacher. "You didn't know, did you?"

"No one told me until now." The impact of this information starts to seep into the depth of Marcia's mind.

"I would guess that half the cast and audiences knew, but you didn't. Wow. I'm sorry, Ms. Johnson."

Marcia gives Anna a hug and thanks her for telling her. Anna peels away to return to her family. A profound sadness overcomes Marcia. She feels she needs to be alone.

KINGDOMS

I'VE BECOME CYNICAL, Malcolm Reid admitted to himself. Early in his career in education, he commuted with older teaching colleagues who would not hide their bitterness about their work in schools. They didn't mind the kids (although a few challenging students buried themselves into their teachers' psyches); they detested the politics of public education. They felt used, abused, and ignored. As a young teacher, Malcolm vowed he would never allow himself to be so negative in the last five years of his career. *But I'm not as cynical as those old guys.*

"What's so earth-shattering that we have to attend this meeting?" asked Malcolm's friend, Lewis Featherstone, also a vice principal. "A new police board protocol? Why? The old one's fine. But here we are. Four cops in uniform, one superintendent, her assistant, principals, vice principals, board employees, and they want to feed us all? What a waste."

"It's a money bomb. The money comes from higher up. The board is spending what it's been given. Read political agenda," Malcolm answered. "I wish that they wouldn't feed us lunch, turn down the lights for video presentations, and then expect us to stay awake."

However, Malcolm remembered that the best principals he'd had were in their last five years of their careers. *Where's Bill Brownland when you need him?* They were the ones who could manage bureaucratic and political agendas. *Dead. Thanks a lot, Bill.* They stood up for students, teachers, and their communities, forging ahead for what was right. They had nothing to lose with little fear of repercussions. Yet their connections could also help them accomplish things that younger principals could not. These people inspired him to become a vice principal with the hope of being a principal.

Malcolm Reid, with less than five years left in his career, had not accomplished his goal of being secondary school principal in the Eutopia School Board. For various reasons known and unknown to him, being principal before retirement would not happen. He became stuck, "not promotable," a career vice principal. To compensate for this, Malcolm considered himself to be a principal, and most principal and vice principal colleagues treated him as such.

"The food is good," Lewis remarked.

"Yes, but lots of carbs. I'm bound to fall asleep," Malcolm lamented. Lewis laughed.

The Eutopia School Board continually reworked policies and practices, seeking constant improvement. Experts had been seconded from schools to work for the board on those revisions. The newest changes required in-servicing at the Eutopia board office.

After a police sergeant spoke briefly, the assistant to the superintendent, Biff Surogatovic, detailed new practice specifically with seizure and storage of illicit drugs.

Lewis leaned over to Malcolm to comment, "How Biff ever got this position, I don't know. He's elementary. What's he know about drugs in high school? Why the hell is he telling us what to do?"

"Because he can. He's a loyal servant of the king," Malcolm quietly responded.

The king in this case was actually a queen, Superintendent Joanna Kerr. She stood beside Surogatovic with her hands folded together, left hand over right, in front of her abdomen. She and her assistant wore navy blue, contributing to a sea of blue alongside police uniforms.

Malcolm Reid yawned while Surogatovic spoke. "The continuity of evidence must be maintained," he explained to a young elementary vice principal who asked a question. "Yes, I know that police don't necessarily come immediately when an administrator calls them about discovery of drugs. They're busy people." Surogatovic looked over to the sergeant, who nodded agreement with that statement. "Keeping drugs locked in a vault overnight does not guarantee that the evidence has not been compromised."

A clarifying question came from Lewis Featherstone. "How would a locked safe not ensure continuity of evidence?" Aware that others' eyes observed Lewis next to him, Malcolm stifled a yawn.

"Who else knows the combination to the school safe?" Surogatovic inquired.

"The head secretary," Featherstone replied.

"See? You can't guarantee that evidence hasn't been tampered with," Surogatovic retorted. He then began to outline what needed to be done differently.

"That's ridiculous," Lewis said sotto voce to Malcolm. "Good thing my head secretary isn't here."

"No kidding," Malcolm concurred. "My head secretary would shoot lasers from her eyes. Then she'd shout victorious war chants. His life would be over."

Surogatovic continued. "Administrators should, when they leave for the day, seal the drugs in an envelope and take them home with them."

Lewis leaned toward Malcolm to ask, "What would the lawyers at Principals' Council say about that?"

The question forced Malcolm to open his eyes. "They'd hate it," he replied. For several years, Malcolm represented secondary administrators in the board, meeting regularly with elementary and secondary representatives from other boards. One of his responsibilities involved disseminating legal advice from council's legal team. Prevention of legal miscalculations spared suffering for administrators and their boards.

Back at school late that afternoon, a sizable drug bust came Mr. Reid's way via a teacher's observation of a student. From Malcolm's investigation and subsequent follow-up, he seized drugs, contacted parents, consulted the principal, notified the assistant superintendent, and left a message for the police officer connected to the school. He departed from the school about 6:30 p.m. Because police were unable to pick up the drugs until the following day, in compliance with board instruction, he sealed them in a large envelope and took them home with him.

Malcolm Reid, anxious to be at home with his wife for a late dinner, applied greater pressure than he should have with his foot on the accelerator pedal of his car. This caught the attention of a police officer that held a radar gun. Another officer farther down the street waved Malcolm over. That officer began the process of writing a speeding ticket.

After preliminaries, Officer Zeller pointed across Malcolm to a brown envelop on the front passenger seat. "What's in that?" she asked.

Malcolm felt sweat sticking his shirt to the back of his car seat. *How should I answer this?* He also wondered if his discomfort might be evident to Officer Zeller. *Well, honesty is the best policy, isn't it?*

After he revealed to her the contents of the envelope, she didn't take it as a joke as he hoped. Instead she remained silent. Malcolm explained his position as it was advised to him at the police board protocol meeting.

"Would you show me the contents of that envelope, please, sir?" Officer Zeller directed.

From his jail cell, Malcolm wished he had his cellular phone because he had personal contact numbers for the legal team from Principals' Council. However, his mobile phone had been confiscated. Passed out on the floor, the drunk next to him had peed his pants, and a puddle formed on the floor, which had crept into the soles of

Malcolm's shoes. The vice principal pondered the events of his day. *This is a nightmare!*

Malcolm felt an elbow in his side. It wasn't the drunk from the jail cell; Lewis Featherstone jarred him back into the police board protocol meeting.

"Did I snore?" Malcolm asked.

"No."

"Did anyone see me sleeping?"

"No. Now I know why you always position yourself in the back row in the corner."

"You got it," Malcolm acknowledged.

"So what are you going to do about this, Mr. Principals' Council Representative?"

"I'll talk to Joanna after the meeting. "I don't want to embarrass her or Surogatovic by raising the issue in this forum."

"Good plan, Councillor."

As soon as the meeting ended, Malcolm spoke with Joanna Kerr. *She has more experience than Biff. She knows what goes on.* She listened carefully. "I'm sure you're aware of the legal difficulty for school administrators here." Before she became superintendent, she worked with Malcolm on the local Principals' Council, so he felt confident that with old knowledge from council work and board legal advice, she would certainly understand.

"This has been vetted through all the channels, Malcolm," she explained.

"Did you consult Principals' Council legal team?" he asked. She didn't answer. "I can do that. I can get an opinion for you."

With a flash of anger in her eyes and voice, Superintendent Kerr inquired, "Are you sicking Principals' Council on me?"

For a second, Malcolm processed her emotional reaction. "No, not at all. The Principals' Council isn't a union. You know that. Principals don't want a union, and they'll never be a union. I'm trying to get a legal opinion that I know would better inform Biff and the committee. I want the best for the board, police, principals, and public education in general. What's wrong with that?"

Kerr replied, "I'm not sure that you're aware, but Biff did a lot of work on this."

Board-wide reputation underlined Joanna Kerr's loyalty to her employees. Now her defence of Biff Surogatovic reinforced it.

She doesn't see the big picture here. Do I intimidate her? I don't think so. "Just so you have another perspective, I'll contact one of the council lawyers this afternoon. It'll be just advice. You can ignore it if you want." Another administrator approached Superintendent Kerr at that moment, so for maintenance of privacy of their conversation, Malcolm told Joanna, "I'll get back to you on that."

Back at school, Malcolm Reid called Sarah Measure, one of the Principals' Council's lawyers. She had developed an international reputation for her expertise in educational law. After explaining the new protocol to her, she concurred with his concerns. "Malcolm, send me a copy of the policy. Things are busy here right now, but I can have an opinion to you in a couple of weeks. I'll send you an email."

True to her word, Malcolm received an email two weeks later from Sarah that disagreed with the new protocol's procedures around continuity of evidence. He forwarded it to Superintendent Joanna Kerr. Gratitude was not her response; she was argumentative and dismissive. She retorted that the board's lawyer advised the committee that created the new protocol. Trustees had approved the new protocol at the last board meeting, and it had become official board procedure. *Usually our board lawyer contacts Sarah Measure because she's the expert.*

I guess not here. Via email, Malcolm thanked Sarah for her work, but he also explained that Superintendent Kerr chose different legal advice. *I did what I could.* Then his thoughts moved into another area: retirement. *Soon, but not soon enough,* he thought with a smile.

In keeping with the continuity of kingdoms, Biff Surogatovic had designs on being a superintendent. This pleased Joanna Kerr because if he became superintendent, she would have greater influence in the board. Their plan included a short placement, just two years, as principal in a lower socioeconomic area of the Eutopia School District. This would round out his portfolio. Everything was going to plan until the second year.

Biff Surogatovic had the misfortune of discovering on school property a large quantity of drugs belonging to one of his grade 8 students. As much as he tried with phone calls and emails to get the police to come before the end of that day, circumstances forced him to follow his own advice on the police board protocol. Rather than leave it in the school's safe, he packed the drugs into a large envelope, sealed it, marked it "DRUGS," and brought it home with him for the weekend.

On a golf course in October, two friends spent time together. Lewis Featherstone updated Malcolm Reid, his recently retired golfing partner, on moves, promotions, and news in the Eutopia board. Malcolm already knew that the Eutopia board moved Lewis to another school in July. "If they kept us in schools for longer periods of time, then students, parents, and staff would gel better with administration," Lewis lamented.

While placing his tee and ball in line with markers for the fourth hole, Malcolm agreed without looking at Lewis. "It's like the superintendents meet in secret with no deep thought. Then they trade administrators like baseball cards."

Suddenly, a thought came to Lewis. "Oh, do you know about Biff Surogatovic?"

"No." Malcolm positioned himself to drive the ball.

"This is a juicy one, but I wouldn't want it to happen to anyone. It's sad, actually," Lewis continued. "Kinda like classical tragedy. Tragic flaw. Hamartia." Malcolm took a practice swing. "Remember that meeting we attended on the new police board protocol where Biff wanted us to take drugs home if police hadn't come to pick up ..."

Malcolm interrupted, "Oh, I remember." With force he drove the ball well and straight at first, but then it curved to the right, landing in the rough. "Crap. Did you see where the ball went?"

"Yeah, we'll find it. Your swing looked fine."

"I see roughly where it went," he stated while he picked up his tee. "So what about Biff?"

Lewis began his routine to drive the ball. "He takes the drugs home, but in the morning, he can't find the envelope. It's gone. Disappeared. Police come to the school, and he tells them he can't find the drugs."

"I bet that went over well with the cops and superintendent," Malcolm deduced.

"Somehow the press caught wind of it. Joanna Kerr looked stressed for the television cameras. They gave her the gears. You didn't hear or read about this?"

Smiling, Malcolm answered, "No. I've been away." *And so glad for that. Can't say I didn't warn them.*

Lewis smiled back. His drive followed the same path as Malcolm's ball. "It's near yours. We'll find them."

"So what happened?"

They returned their clubs to their golfing bags. "Finally, the truth emerged. Biff's son, a high school senior, found at home an envelope with "DRUGS" written on it, so he had a party with it with friends."

"Oh, that's no good," Malcolm reacted with a straight face. A pause followed. Lewis looked at Malcolm. Silence. Then Malcolm exploded with laughter. Lewis followed his lead. "Karma, Lewis. That's karma."

"Yes, indeed." They hooted for another half minute. "Instead of drinks on the nineteenth hole, how about just desserts?" They cackled more.

Malcolm put his right arm on Lewis's shoulder and asked, "How long before you retire?"

WHAT'S A FOOT?

DEAR CHERYL,

I share this tale with you because it's true, and it applies to you. It's partly my story, but mostly it's about an old boyfriend of mine. You're now in a similar situation to him years ago. Please know that you are my first prayer in my day, and throughout the day, I yearn for your complete healing. I'm sharing details about me that you may not want to know (Sorry!), but they reveal more about his character than mine. That's why you must know this account of determination, forbearance, endurance, and hope. I can't tell you this in person, so I'll have your mother read it to you.

I was in love with Joe our last year of high school at Eutopia Central High School. Many people wondered what attracted me to him, including your mom. Lots of girls wanted to be with him. Yes, he was a brash, conceited, cocky, competitive captain of the basketball team—tall, dark, and handsome. I was a quiet girl who discovered acting as means to counterbalance introversion. Joe wasn't just a jock; he also had talents in art, especially in painting and sculpture, with enhanced vision his creations expressed boldness, confidence, and appreciation. I still have a painting he gave me of birds in flight.

We both were sprinters on the Eutopia Central track and field team, but Joe also ran middle distance because he developed endurance. Joe found me attractive, and that was gratifying. All his

WHAT'S A FOOT?

faults that others saw remained invisible to me by choice. I have always loved without analysis. Humans are complicated, but I don't believe in keeping ledgers in relationships. I saw only Joe's good qualities, and to this day, they are all that matter to me.

When I first started to date him, your mom said to me, "Sparrow, you know something? Joe can be an ass. He's going to use you and hurt you like he has everyone else."

"Not me," I told her. "I'm pretty level-headed. Besides, if we break up, maybe I dump him and break his heart." Your mom laughed, and that ended her concern.

One trait of Joe's rose above other laudable qualities. "Limits don't hinder me," he would say with a smile. "They challenge me." His sense of adventure and zest for life drew me to him. In track, his personal best times became history with regularity. His fixation for perfection pressed him to new standards. In his mind, the word *impossible* did not exist.

Joe aspired to be a commercial pilot, and he neared completion of his private pilot's licence. One day he surprised me. He had his friend fly us for a stunning, panoptic view over Eutopia. Then he handed me a parachute and said, "Come on, Sparrow. Let's jump." I didn't have time to be scared. I trusted Joe. He desired to share intimately his gifts of exploration and spontaneity with me, and I chose not to fear, but to accept. After a quick lesson, we lunged from the plane and flew. It felt natural, joyful. That experience intensified my gravitation to him. I was literally falling in love.

My brother worried that Joe's motorcycle was too small and dangerous with two people on it. "Just saying," he warned me. I remember my dad shaking Joe's hand at each encounter, often with his pipe in his left hand. He returned to puffing after the handshake. My mom made sure we had our helmets on tightly, wishing us safety each time we left on that Honda.

He used to hotdog on that motorbike with me on it. It was fun. However, the day before our high school graduation, he was going too fast and hit something on the road, and we went flying. That's all I remember of that day.

I broke my right femur, pelvic bone, clavicle, and right arm. I suffered a concussion, dislocated my shoulder, and suffered some road rash. I remained in hospital for the summer, which provided time for self-reflection, lessons in patience, and healing by determination.

In much worse shape than me, Joe was on life support with a broken neck, shattered mouth, brain and spinal cord damage, broken bones, and significant loss of blood. Doctors believed he wouldn't survive the first night, yet somehow he did. They kept saying that for two weeks. His parents told me this when they visited me.

Within a few days of the accident, the early stages of healing permitted me, with assistance from nurses via wheelchair, to see Joe. He remained in a coma. His parents were there daily, praying over him. They prayed for me too.

After news spread about our accident, high school friends stopped by to visit Joe and me. If they saw him first, their shock carried over to me, and I had to cheer them up. If they came to see me first, I warned them about the severity of his injuries. After their initial visits, many came only to see me. Joe's condition near death upset them.

Then, to everyone's amazement, about four weeks after the accident, Joe came out of the coma. He couldn't talk, but he could hear, and he could communicate with his eyes—one blink for yes and two blinks for no.

After I left hospital as a patient, I returned for visits. He knew me. He turned his head to see me. Joe blinked for me. With his limitations, we only communicated about his physical feelings. Because I guided our conversation, I avoided talking about our relationship. I still don't know why.

He'd never talk again, the experts said, but he did.

His mouth moved, and he uttered groans. With that development, his parents persuaded the medical team to have his mouth reconstructed. After several surgeries, his communication improved. Speech pathology accompanied them, but even with advancements, he spoke with tortured sluggishness. That was when I lost control of our conversations. He began to speak about us. I wasn't ready for that.

I started college by then. I had almost fully healed and was making new friends. I wasn't connected to Joe in the same way as before. Life opened new perspectives and opportunities. My visitations with Joe happened less often. He voiced his discontent with that a few times, once with resentment. Good fortune had it that students and staff from high school compensated for my absence. They lifted Joe's spirit, and they inspired him to overcome. That was what he told me. Equally, they confessed that he boosted their lives.

That's not to say Joe didn't have down days or even weeks of depression. For one stretch of time, he believed that death would have been the preferable outcome of our accident. With vehemence I disagreed. That was when his healing halted. He snapped out of it through empathetic friends and family who uplifted, prayed, reassured, and lauded his progress. Advancement in his physical condition returned. Somehow these things held him together—that, and his desire to master his competitor, his broken body. "I'm going to win," he often said, as if he were coaching and motivating himself.

In the early stages of his recovery during physiotherapy, on occasion frustration led to anger. However, he soon realised and accepted the futility of that, so his outbursts stopped. Perhaps in the absence of rage, Joe began to display increasing determination and patience. If he had doubts, he never voiced them. Where did his strength come from? Again, those daily visits from family and friends and their prayers sustained him.

"He won't walk again," the experts said.

"They're wrong," Joe declared to me. "Remember in track when we were training, and we'd get a stitch? And Coach said, 'Run through it'?"

"Yes."

"Well, this time in my life is just a stitch, and I'm gonna run through it." He made me laugh.

I met Tom near the end of my first year in college. With patience, knowing the complicated feelings I had for Joe, he kept me company. Tom's gentleness and steadiness drew me closer to him. He guided me through my healing. I learned to trust Tom, and I fell in love with him. Guilt about waning feelings for Joe accompanied my increasing attraction to Tom. Still, I knew that I had to tell Joe. What would that do to him? I thought that in some way, I had been part of his improvements. Would telling him the truth set things back and stop his progress? Finding the right moment to confess weighed heavily on me.

Instead, Joe initiated conversation on the subject. "Seeing you lately, I've realised that something's been missing. It's not as though I haven't had time to think about this. I have. Lots. It's been painful. I'm sure you sensed it." He paused. "Our love isn't what it used to be. That isn't anyone's fault. It's just what is." Somehow, intuition led him to free me. "Who can hold a Sparrow?" he joked while a tear ran down his face.

Joe wanted me to have freedom, but he still desired me as a friend. I cried because he removed from me the burden of first confessing my love for Tom. That liberated me. Joe's straightforwardness wrapped in gentleness wasn't a typical break-up. Perhaps Joe knew about Tom. However, from that moment on, Joe and I transitioned from a romance to a lasting friendship. I began to bring Tom with me to visit Joe. They became friends. Everyone liked Joe, and Joe liked everyone. His joy of living and charm drew people to him.

For about two months after our break-up, Joe was moody. People noticed his motivation wavered. He had down days, but they didn't occur back-to-back. Guilt badgered me because I attributed this to the change in our relationship. Yet, Joe told me toward the end of this season of sullenness that my suspicion about the cause was unfounded. He was conscious of his moods, and he was working toward being his normal self. He claimed that he remained positive about how things changed between us. He had support from friends and family, but he also sought advice from professional counsellors. Your mother told me that you have done likewise. Good for you.

Ms. Marcia Johnson, my dramatic arts teacher, and Mr. Hal Stratton, Joe's chemistry teacher and basketball coach, came to see Joe one day while Tom and I were there. They informed us that two basketball scholarships for graduating students had been established at Eutopia Central High School in Joe's honour. That news brought so much joy to him. His eyes and voice beaconed his delight.

Now able to move in a wheelchair, Joe made friends with other patients on the same hospital floor. He visited them and lifted their spirits. He became a motivator, an inspiration for others there with serious physical infirmities. Then he was sent home to live with his parents.

During his subsequent physiotherapy, Joe pushed himself and others, facilitating his transition from wheelchair to walking. Over several months, he accomplished that objective, although it required a walker to assist him.

"I'm going to walk without a walker," Joe told me with his reconstructed smile. "You'll see." Then he surprised me. "I'm going back to high school."

"What?" I paused. "Why? You graduated already."

"But I can't remember most of it. Chemistry? Zippo. Math? Nada. Physics? Partial. I have to relearn it just like I've had to relearn how to walk."

"Have you asked how to do that—going back to school?" I asked.

He answered, "Mr. Stratton looked into it for me. I'm returning to Eutopia Central High School in September." That stunned me.

His return to high school began with him alternating between a wheelchair and a walker. Part of his day involved assisting in various senior associated classrooms, which included physically disabled, Down syndrome, mentally handicapped, and multiple-exceptionality students.

"He's their hero," Ms. Johnson told me. "They look up to him and call out to him when they see him in the hall. He recognises their worth by returning their greetings. He loves them, and they love him. He is so positive with everyone. His example is affirmative and infectious. He makes Eutopia Central a better place."

I saw Joe less often as I neared graduation. When I did see him, he had advanced from use of a wheelchair and walker to walking with a cane. I noticed that on my own, but he insisted on emphasising his accomplishment. "Look at me. I'm walking with a cane," he said with his slow speech and wide smile. "But I'm going to walk without it; I swear." I congratulated him. "Watch," he instructed. Joe pointed to his right foot, which, while he promenaded, revealed an abnormal landing on the ground, levelling only when his weight forced his foot to flatten. When he lifted that foot, it returned to its tilted position with his instep higher than the exterior of his foot. His muscles on his foot and calf, despite physiotherapy, had not returned to normal.

Showing conviction and no emotion, Joe stated, "If this foot can't work the way I want without a cane, I'm going to amputate it." That stunned me, but it did not astonish me. Joe's determination guided him. What was a foot, considering what he had been through?

The next time I saw him, Tom and I told him that we were engaged. He congratulated us. Then Joe pointed to his right foot. "Here's another announcement—a good one too. I want to show you something." He lifted his pant leg to reveal a prosthetic. "See? I told you." He paraded before us. "No cane. I can walk just fine now. I'd rather go through life without a foot than be limited. I want to be unlimited."

That's Joe: optimistic, dedicated, determined, and boundless.

One unforeseen consequence of Joe's accident was how it directed the lives of his friends. I became a nurse, your mother a physiotherapist, Tom a neurologist, Brenda (another Eutopia Central High School classmate) an occupational therapist, Hannah (another former girlfriend of Joe's) a psychologist, and Brad (Joe's basketball teammate) an orthopaedic surgeon. Joe and his accident led us to healing, not only our own and Joe's, but also the world around us. Joe inspired us.

He's also the one who kept contact with all his high school friends. Joe has been the glue that held us together. Everyone has Joe as a friend on social media. He holds parties every year during Christmas season and summer. They are well attended and enjoyed. His love for others is contagious.

That's why I write this story for you, Cheryl. Knowing your mother as I do, she is no doubt crying while she reads this to you. I'm sending Joe to visit you soon. He will inspire you and give you hope. You will hear him say, "I am unlimited." He will tell you that you are unlimited too. Healing is within grasp, and when it comes, you will use your talents to develop new ones—ones you never knew that you had. Your gift to this world is you.

With love,
Sparrow

BREAKING BULL BROWN

WE'VE BEEN FRIENDS, Bull and I, since kindergarten in North Eutopia. Bull's parents owned the feed store, and my parents grew crops. People said we were inseparable. We've been tighter than brothers. We see things the same, and we love each other. The only person dearer has been my wife, Janine.

As teenagers, he dated my wife, and I dated his. We were best men at each other's wedding. Our kids are named after Bull (Bill) and Christina. Their kids are named Ryan and Janine, after us. That's how close our friendship has been.

He became Bull instead of Bill from rodeo, a passion he had as a young kid until college. His energy and drive have been incomparable. As a capitalist, Bull demonstrated success, multiplying assets to the family business. He was always a good communicator; Bull had a natural way of speaking to people one-on-one and in a crowd. Always charismatic, he was a pied piper, and all us rats would follow Bull anywhere.

About four years ago, when Bull, Christine, Janine, and I hired a babysitter and were driving to a movie together, Janine and Bull argued about education.

"You want to tear it apart," Janine accused Bull.

"I want to repair it. I want accountability and transparency. I want kids to learn without waste and politics inherent in education," Bull explained with hints of passion in his voice. "Look, Janine. If you really want to protect public schools, why don't you run for trustee?" Janine looked stunned. Other than the music on the radio (It was "Turn Me Loose" by Loverboy), the car went silent for ten seconds. "Are you thinking about it?" he continued.

Janine responded, "Yes. I'd be an excellent trustee. Still, I'm the mother of two young children. I work full time and care for a particularly needy child, namely my husband, Ryan. That takes all my energy and time." That elicited laughter at my expense, but I didn't mind. I wouldn't want Janine to become a trustee. That was more time away from our kids and me. I agreed with her. Janine concluded, "I can't be a trustee right now."

"But maybe in the future?" Bull asked.

"Maybe. If circumstances were right." After a shorter pause, she asked Bull, "Why don't you run for trustee?"

Without hesitation Bull replied, "Ditto. My answer is the same as yours." We kidded him about being the mother of two children, but then the three of us ganged up on him. Over the last few years, his constant complaints about taxes and spending in the school system led us to this ultimatum: shut up, or do something about it. That night our dare, coaxing, and appeal to altruism led him to enter politics. We promised to support him for trustee.

With his experience, sagacity, and promise of reform, people in our ward elected Bull to the Eutopia board of education. Finally, the right person would transform an unwieldy bureaucracy into a business. Bull anticipated the ride of his life.

Bull attended an orientation session for new trustees. At his house over a beer, he told me about it. "They explained what the role is, and how much and when we get paid. Then we were paired with a returning or former trustee and rotated around the room every fifteen minutes to different topics."

"Did you give them hell, Bull?" I asked.

"Too soon for that, Ryan. Everyone in the room knows where I stand on issues. There was a lot of fawning. That's a good sign. They're scared of me."

"Glad you saw it for what it was. Stick to your principles, Bull," said I. "You'll make Eutopia school board a model of efficiency. I know it."

At his first board meeting, he asked questions of everyone who presented. The chair let him make mistakes. With his ignorance on stage, he found patient, informative responses from paid staff and fellow trustees. Anticipating a grilling, money managers came fully prepared with facts and figures for Bull. Another trustee reminded the chamber that Bull Brown described himself as a redneck during the election. Bull chuckled and continued with questions, catching some off guard, so they promised to have answers for the next board meeting. He survived the encounter, but he met measured respect and resolved resistance. In hindsight, although he should have been better prepared, Bull established that change was coming to the Eutopia school district.

After that meeting, several people approached him, so I listened while they did. His supporters came first, mostly to congratulate and encourage him further. Others introduced themselves, yet their motives were unclear to me. One woman waited patiently to the end for an audience with Bull. I recognised her but couldn't remember her name.

"Hello Mr. Brown. I'm Cara Zeal. I teach at …"

"Call me, Bull, Cara. Pleased to meet you." His hand stretched forward and Cara's met his for a handshake. "And this is Ryan Golden." I shook her hand too.

She smiled and fondly held on to my hand for longer than I was comfortable. "Yes. I taught your daughter, Christina, three years ago. She's such an exemplary student in the school. No doubt you're proud of her." I accepted her compliment with gratitude. Ms. Zeal let go and turned to Bull. "Bull, I'm wondering if you can come to our school to visit our students. We're in your ward."

Bull responded immediately, "I'd love to come to Eutopia Memorial Elementary School."

"My principal will be excited about your visit." They talked further about the school. Details of Bull's appointment were to be arranged by her principal.

"That's where our kids go," Bull told Cara.

"I know. Somehow, I haven't taught them yet," she replied.

Later—perhaps a little too late for a fresh start to the next day—at my place with beer, we discussed what happened that night.

"Oh, yeah, they want to stay status quo, and I expected that," Bull told me. "But I can't change the culture by myself. Ryan, I'm alone on that board. I'm the only reformer. And it's also going to take time to turn them around."

"What if they turn you around?" I asked. "What if they break you, Bull, just like a bronc?" We looked at each other intently. "You need to be wary, buddy."

"That ain't gonna happen," Bull replied with a smile. We clicked our beer bottles together. "Cheers."

"Cheers," I responded. I still had doubts.

After the next monthly public board meeting just before Christmas, Bull and I snacked at Finnegan's Sports Pub. We conversed about events that evening. He added, "Since that visit at Eutopia

Memorial Elementary School, now all the schools in my ward want me to come."

"I meant to ask you. How did that go?"

"Oh, fine. Cara Zeal had me read to her class. Christina joined me too. We're going to get out of our offices and make early Wednesday afternoons our date spot for reading to kids. Cara's a good teacher. The visit went exceedingly well."

I joked, "So you're not the enemy of the schools, as Trustee Williams has named you. No picket signs when you entered?"

"No, Ryan. They welcomed me. Those kids melt my heart. I tell you, there was one little girl, Ursula, who wants me to read with her every week. I told her and Cara that I would."

"Good for you. Doing your part to improve literacy scores?" I joshed, to no reaction. Bull changed subjects to the game on the big screen, and my eggnog turned somewhat bilious.

From that second board meeting, Bull stirred a bee's nest. He interrogated staff and trustees about contracts for school computer equipment, software, and service. Eventually, the board's purchasing agent quit, though not because she did anything wrong—overtly. Board staff rallied behind her, but Bull, with supportive reporting from local press, wore down her and the others. Her "integrity has been questioned, and that's unacceptable," she claimed when she left. Yet the computer portion of the board's proposed budget dropped by 15 percent the next year without complaints.

Fellow supporter Georgette Temple commented at a ward meeting that Bull held at the Legion Hall. "That's great, Bull. Keep going. Tear the whole Utopia board apart and build it back again proper, like it's supposed to be." Then others there paraded a litany of complaints about the board, individual teachers, unions, and education in general.

Bull altered the tone of that meeting by insisting people file purely professional complaints about individual teachers through proper channels. He didn't want teachers publicly flogged. "Denigrating the teaching profession does nothing for the profession or the students. Support teachers. They help our kids. Let's build morale in schools. Tearing down teachers in general is counter-productive. Hell, I'm a politician, and look what public loathing has done for us." The crowd laughed, except for a few whose body language, facial expressions, and quiet comments indicated that their hero had just betrayed them.

Bull and Christina had been visiting Cara Zeal's grade 3 class weekly. He would read with Ursula, who had a learning disability. Her mother was a single parent with two other children and two jobs. Ursula's supportive extended family didn't see developing her literacy skills as part of their responsibility. Her teachers and educational assistants extended their commitment to her, but something about Ursula drew Bull to her. Christina volunteered with a boy named Rex, whose dyslexia limited his success.

Over dinner, Bull, Christina, Janine, and I talked about the board. At one point, Bull put down his fork and stopped eating. He said, "I've encountered a catch-22 scenario, and I don't know what to do about it. Can you give me some advice?"

"Sure," Janine offered while she poked at her salad. "What happened?"

"I've looked into staff cuts. There are contractual agreements with unions of course, but if we negotiate cuts to educational assistants that I propose, then the Ursulas and Rexes in this board will suffer. I'm conflicted."

Janine reached for her glass of wine and downed some before she spoke. "So you don't want to be the tough guy anymore?"

Bull defended himself. "No. I want our costs down, and I'm working on that. However, since we've been working with Ursula and Rex, I see what cuts can do to kids who need more help than say, our own kids, who learn without problems. There are students in every school who need more help than others. Teachers can only do so much, with emphasis now on individual learning. Our volunteering helps, but if we're only available for an hour a week, Ursula's progress is limited. She needs more help than I can give. Ursula and Rex are doing better, but it's not just because Christina and I help. Educational assistants augment what teachers do in the classroom. What happens to students with learning disabilities if we eliminate the people who help them?"

Janine asked, "Can I come with you and Christine for your next visit with Ursula and Rex? I'd like to see it for myself."

Bull answered, "Sure. I'll talk to the principal and get back to you."

We resumed eating, and Janine started a new topic. "By the way, Bull, people are talking about you bringing Junior Achievement to North Eutopia. They're excited."

With enthusiasm, Bull stabbed his empty fork upward into the air. "Yes! Me too! Let's encourage more business people, entrepreneurs. I'm pumped!"

Christina added, "Here's something special. On the upcoming Professional Development Day, Bull and I are bringing Rex and Ursula and their parents to a session on the reading program at Eutopia Memorial. Along with Cara Zeal, we're presenting to teachers from schools throughout the Eutopia board. They're comparing successes and disappointments with reading programs in their schools."

Janine and I glanced at each other and then at Christina and Bull. Their excitement lived in their visages. "That's excellent," Janine commented.

With treats for my children, I dropped by Eutopia Memorial. (It was cake, but lunch had just finished.) The office wouldn't let me deliver them in person, but the secretary assured me that at the recess break, they would be called down to the office to receive them. Then

BREAKING BULL BROWN

Bull and Christina appeared in the office. The secretary informed them that Cara Zeal was on her way with Rex and Ursula.

While we waited, I asked them about two books they held. "This one is for Rex," explained Christina. It was *Yes, This Is My First Rodeo* by Megan Alexander. The other, meant for Ursula, was *Cowboy Cody* by Becky Wigemyr. "Both the kids have taken an interest in rodeo, so we found them these."

When the kids arrived, their delight with and gratitude for the gifts were spontaneous. "I love rodeo!" Ursula declared. The kids hugged Bull and Christina. "Can we read these now?" Ursula asked. I began to understand more fully their connection to my friends.

"Oh, yes. Of course," Bull replied. "How was your testing this morning?"

Ursula lowered her head. "It was okay." Cara Zeal shook her head without Ursula or Rex seeing their teacher's contradictory gesture.

Rex answered, "I'm glad it's over."

Zeal instructed, "Rex and Ursula, why don't you walk to the library with those books and wait for Mr. and Mrs. Brown to join you there? I want to talk to them for a moment." The children complied.

"Good to see you, Mr. Golden," Zeal said while shaking my hand. "Are you volunteering to read to students too?"

"No, just dropping off things for my kids, and then I ran into these two."

She directed her attention to the Browns. "It wasn't easy. Ursula ran out of time. Rex had difficulty staying on task." She looked at me and then returned to them. "I can't show you their tests, but I can show you a blank copy of last year's test, if you'd like to talk about standardised testing after your sessions today."

"Christina can't, but I will," Bull informed her.

At Finnegan's Sports Pub, with reference to that encounter in the school office, I asked Bull about standardised testing. He replied,

"What a waste of money and time." I must have shown shock. "I mean, literacy scores, testing, et cetera," he clarified. Then his glance returned to hockey on the big screen.

This seemed uncharacteristic of him. Why? If he advocated accountability throughout the system, then surely tests of students' math, literacy, science, and technology competencies were essential. I proclaimed his inconsistency.

With his salsa-covered index finger pointing at me for emphasis, Bull replied, "Accountability is not the goal. Standardised testing justifies everyone's job from government on down to the board. Testing legitimises the bureaucracy. It does little for teaching and learning."

This puzzled me further. "How does it legitimise the bureaucracy?"

"It increases the size and scope of bureaucracy. If we want to cut costs and make a smaller bureaucracy, we should get rid of it. But that's beyond the board's control. I can't change that locally."

"Okay, explain yourself," I insisted.

Bull grinned as he continued. "To improve test results, governments and boards spend valuable time and resources so that teachers and students master the test. Yet it doesn't show the full picture of students' knowledge and abilities. Standardised testing narrows knowledge and the capabilities of students. It's like taking a photo with a macro lens for an extreme close-up instead of a wide-angle lens for a broader picture."

I stopped eating nachos. "I'm totally surprised at you saying that."

"Oh, my views are not popular."

"Even I don't agree with you, Bull. You're beginning to sound like the teachers' union."

"I've learned this from asking questions in conversations with a variety of people," Bull continued. "There's another problem with standardised testing. It's a snapshot in time. Like any test, it's only as good as the day of testing. If kids are hungry, worried about things at home, anxious about the test, sick with a cold, bullied, or insecure, then results will not be indicative of the child's full potential. Take Ursula for instance." He dipped a chicken wing in sauce.

Bull gingerly returned the wing from his mouth to his plate. "Oh, this sauce is a little hotter than I expected," Bull commented. He reached for a serviette and wiped his mouth. "Her test results are awful. But outside of pressure to perform on standardised tests, she reads well with comprehension. She's managing her disability. She's improving." He took a sip of water.

"You and I know standardised testing is here to stay. So how do you get her to perform better on standardised testing?"

"If the testing had application in her life, the survivalist that she is, she could teach the testers many things. Instead, they ask her theoretical, abstract questions about readings that have no correlation to her life. Her teacher knows how to mine Ursula's talents in the classroom, but the test designers haven't considered her individual strengths." Bull dipped a second wing more carefully in the hot sauce.

We talked further about the Eutopia board that night. Instead of criticism, he was ebullient in his view about several innovations, cooperation, and accomplishments in the board.

What happened to my friend? He used to be so critical of education in our district and beyond. He was anti-union. He was for more accountability and less spending. Yet he became friendly with trustees and they with him, even Trustee Williams, who had damned him earlier. Perhaps staff stroked his ego, charmed him, and blinded him. Maybe the unions treated him to dinner. I didn't know. Bull lost his edge. We wanted him to change the deep state, but that wasn't happening.

I told him exactly how I felt because I knew Bull Brown appreciated frankness. "They got to you, Bull. They bamboozled you. As a lion, you've lost your roar. You've lost your values. You wanted to make education in this area leaner, meaner, and better. Now, you're one of them, one of the entrenched."

I hoped he would have become angry, defensive, or even remorseful, but he didn't. Instead, he put down the bones from his chicken wing, picked up another one, and fully dipped it in hot sauce. "I think I'm used to the hotness now. Sure, it's spicy, but it has flavour, and I like it." He placed the entire wing in his mouth. He didn't react to the heat from the wing or me.

I commented to Janine one night as we prepared for bed about Bull's acquiescence since his election. She responded, "I get it. That little girl, Ursula, the one he reads with weekly, is a powerful reminder of the responsibility he has as a trustee. So is Rex."

"How do you know?" I asked.

Janine pulled down her nightgown and brushed her hair. "I've been there. I saw them read to Ursula and Rex." She lifted the sheets on her side of the bed and slipped under them. "It's cute. It's almost as though Ursula leads Bull around by the nose. She's a charmer. He follows her with joy wherever she wants to go. Ursula has a bond with Bull. Rex has a bond with Christina."

"I'm trying to picture that: big Bull and little Ursula."

She adjusted her hair on the pillow. "Those two needy children remind them of the hopes they have for their own kids. They're committed to everyone's kids." Janine paused to choose her words. "In a china shop, profitable change requires tactful analysis, planning, and redesign rather than just letting the bull loose in it."

I snickered at her joke and slipped under the covers to join her. "But Bull's still in the china shop. He needs to be a bull."

She faced me with intense sincerity. "Ryan, Bull's changed what should be changed and preserved what needed preserving. He does what he can. That will disappoint some, but he's been a good trustee." She turned onto her back. "By the way, I'm volunteering to read once a week with a girl named Flower." She leaned to turn out her lamp on the night table. "Good night."

Six months before the next election for trustee, Bull announced through the media that he would not seek re-election. It surprised his supporters, board trustees and staff, and most of all me. We wondered why. He seemed to enjoy success in the role he adopted. He went from redneck to respected representative. True, he didn't accomplish everything his supporters wanted, but he did make changes. How the Eutopia board did things improved, and that helped us as critics to believe more in public education in our area.

Bull and Christina invited Janine and me to their place after his announcement. After two glasses of wine before dinner, Janine asked why he quit.

"I'm a businessman, not a politician. A second term would mean I'm a politician," he replied. "I'll still have my contacts with schools through reading and Junior Achievement."

Janine continued with her words, slurring slightly. "But you were good at it, Bull. You know so much more than you did before you were first elected. Change your mind. Be a trustee again."

Christina snickered. "Bull, change his mind? You're kidding, right?"

Then Bull spoke with misty earnestness. "Sometimes it's even been fun, but I've learned that being a trustee is only one way to support good public education. What we do with kids is an investment in the future. Students, parents, neighbours, volunteers, staff, coaches, politicians—we're all in it together." He stared ahead in silence and then uttered, "You should run for office, Janine."

"No, I couldn't," she responded. "Not me."

"Why not?" I asked. "You'd be good at it."

Janine waved back and forth her third glass of wine in synchronisation with her head. "No, no, no!" Some wine spilled, and we laughed.

Bull stated, "Good. It's settled then. Janine will run." Bull paused. "We'll support you along the way."

So that was how Janine became a trustee for the Eutopia District School Board.

INDULGENCE

AFTER SHE PAID for her coffee and muffin, Carla turned around to scan the coffee shop for an empty table. The only one was in the back corner next to the glassed barrier by the entryway. She pulled a couple of paper serviettes from a dispenser on the counter. During her walk to her destination, she sensed benign, innocent surveillances from most of the patrons there. However, one hostile scrutiny tracked Carla to where she sat down by herself.

She prepared the coffee lid, removed the muffin's paper wrapping, and pulled her cell phone from her purse. Work didn't require her until eleven o'clock, so this leisurely start to the day and break from her routine gave her delight. However, one distracting feature of her indulgence there came from the table next to Carla: two women having a conversation. One woman was unapologetically loud—the same one whose stare condemned her and her race as she sat down next to them at the only empty table. Carla reminded herself: *Is her problem dat, nuh mine.* Sometimes Carla's internal thoughts reverted to her dialect from childhood, especially in situations that raised her ire.

In an English accent, this bulky woman boomed with ostensible obliviousness, "Now, I'll admit. My son, Jason, is no angel. He has a few self-control issues, I'll grant you, but if people knew his good points, talents, and heart, they would love him as I do. The problem Jason and I face together is this stupid educational system, namely the

Eutopia School District. What an inflexible and ineffective school board it is, I can tell you. They don't have patience for Jason. He can't get a fresh start in each of the schools that he has been transferred to. He is marked as soon as he arrives. No one gives him a chance. I'm tired of it." Jason's mother drank from her coffee cup.

Carla tried to focus on her phone, but this woman's overwhelming voice distracted her. She looked around the coffee shop to see if others had vacated their tables. *No such luck,* she thought. *Others seem to ignore her. How do they do it?*

The larger woman continued, "You know what he's like in Cadets. He's a model cadet. He has the respect of those younger ones. He's a natural leader."

The smaller woman confirmed in a far less voluminous voice, "Yes. Jason's good at giving marching orders. He has a strong voice like you, Gilda."

Gilda. Gilda, I can't even hear myself think. Yet Carla could not activate enough courage to confront Gilda with her complaint.

"Iris, he's a natural-born leader. Major Entwhistle encouraged Jason to enlist," Gilda crowed. "At Cadets, he's happy, involved, appreciated …"

Iris interjected, "But not so much at school, eh?"

Gilda leaned into the table to emphasise to her primary audience her feelings on the issue. "Do you know how many meetings I've attended where I'm told the same things about Jason?" The other woman shook her head. "Too many to count. Cadets can engage him. Why can't the schools?"

Carla stopped pretending to read the news on her phone. Gilda's pronouncements reminded Carla of problems her son, Zeke, also had in high school. *He's still not completely through that yet. But I know the school's been doing the best it can. And so has Zeke.*

Gilda griped further, "We left South Eutopia because of the schools and moved up here, but the same problems are here too. It's wrong, Iris. I'm going to fix that if it's the last thing I do."

I'd rather live up north here too. It's too crowded in South Eutopia—too many distractions and temptations for the kids. Carla nibbled a piece of her blueberry muffin.

Iris asked Gilda, "So why is he home today?"

"Suspension. That's all they ever do."

Iris sought clarification. "And that's at the alternative school, right?'

"Not much of an alternative, if you ask me," Gilda replied. "They're meeting right now at the school today to discuss Jason's situation."

"Who are they?"

"The vice principal, board psychologist, his teacher, his social worker, and the police, but not me. I'm not invited. They're making decisions about my son, and I'm not invited. Can you believe that?" Gilda complained.

"Why'd you move Jason to the alternative school?" Iris wondered.

Carla considered what Gilda might say next. *She didn't move him, is my guess. The school board did.*

"The North Eutopia High School administration has no sense of humour. Jason was only kidding. Everyone took it far too seriously," Gilda proclaimed.

Carla tried not to smile. *I would say Iris don't know the truth. I wonder what Gilda not telling her. From my experience, the primary concern of the staff of North Eutopia High is safety not only for my Zeke but every student in that school. I wonder what her precious Jason did?*

Iris put down her coffee and with a barely audible voice leaned into Gilda, "But, Gilda, people take threats seriously. He can't threaten to kill everyone in the school. Someone has to respond to that. If it's a joke, it's in bad taste. And if it's said in anger, he needs to find control. Think about how the rest of us feel. My Penny goes there too."

With eyes focused on her phone, Carla pressed the email icon. She seemed focused on her own business, and the smile on her face may have reinforced that to others in the coffee shop. *Yes, Iris. Tell her for me!*

The large lady replied, "Now Iris, don't be silly. You know Jason. He's incapable of that." Iris did not retort. "Jason is very excited about his visit with the recruiter next week. How about Penny? Is she interested in joining the armed forces?"

What is dis I'm hearing, though? A boy who want to kill everybody in the school, and want to join the military?!

Iris sipped her coffee and placed her cup on the table before she spoke. "Penny's not interested in joining. In fact, she's not sure she wants to continue in Cadets. I've encouraged her to stick with it, and she has so far. How much longer she'll stick with it, I don't know."

There's no way he could ever represent this country. And then give him a gun? No one in the forces is interested in that. They want people who live with discipline, who serve. They have standards.

Iris looked around to see whether anyone was listening. Others were engaged in conversations of their own, and Carla seemed occupied with her phone. After leaning in again with a quiet voice, Iris asked as discreetly as possible, "Why's Jason suspended now from the alternative school?"

This time, Gilda spoke with less volume after a pause, "Same thing. An overreaction, I'm telling you."

She nuh seeing a pattern here? Carla's eyes abandoned her phone and examined Gilda. That lasted until Gilda, perhaps intuiting Carla's assessment, turned to stare at Carla. Although Carla's eyes retreated sideways for a second, they refocused with determination not to be intimidated by Gilda's glare. Their eyes remained deadlocked until Gilda looked beyond them. Carla coached herself through the discomfort. *I'm feeling judgement and a hint of hate here.* Carla chose to smile. With intentional strategy, her attention returned to her phone. However, the heat of Gilda's glare remained on her. *If looks could kill ...*

Iris inquired, "What's Jason doing now?"

"He's at home, slogging on some school work that they've provided. But it's all wrong. He needs individual attention from a teacher. How can he work at home alone and understand what he's supposed to know?"

Maybe he shouldn't threaten to kill people. Then he wouldn't be suspended. Then he can have all the individual attention from his teacher that he needs.

"Iris, Penny does some tutoring, right?" Gilda asked.

"Yes."

"Do you think she can help Jason with his English assignment?"

Carla looked up to gauge Iris's reaction. "She's really busy right now, Gilda. I don't want her to overcommit. She's got so much on her plate."

"Ask her, could you, please? Jason needs help," Gilda asserted.

Jason sound like a sociopath. I think him need a whole heap of help. Carla looked down because a text from her son, Zeke, came her way, but she had enough of a glimpse of Iris's reaction to know that she wasn't happy about Gilda's bidding.

Iris gulped her coffee before answering. "Okay, I'll ask, but I know how overwhelmed she feels right now. Just saying."

"Thanks. You know how indebted I'll be when she helps Jason."

Zeke's text read, "I need you to pick me up at school, now."

Carla replied on her phone, "What happened?"

Iris stood and gulped the remainder of her coffee. "Thanks for the coffee and visit, Gilda."

"You're welcome. We'll have to do it again, soon." Gilda cradled her coffee as Iris exited the coffee shop.

"Now, Mom! Now!"

Panic crept into Carla's thoughts. She dictated her response to the phone. "Tell me what's happening. I'm eight minutes from the school."

In reaction to her voice, Gilda now turned her attention again to Carla, scolding her. "Hey, can you keep it down? Some of us are trying to have a peaceful cup of coffee in here." Carla didn't hear her because she concentrated on communication with her son.

Zeke sent a text with the following message: "Inzsqwweertml."

"What's going on?" Carla spoke into her cell phone. It was then that a siren blasted its warning as a police cruiser spun its tires out of the coffee shop's parking lot. This compounded her anxiety. "Just go to the office," Carla continued. She checked her message before sending it. In the next few seconds while she waited for Zeke's reply, Carla considered several ominous situations. No message came. She gathered her things and exited.

"Thanks for taking your conversation outside," Gilda jettisoned with sarcasm when Carla rushed by her.

In her vehicle, Carla attempted to remain calm, which allowed memories to return: Zeke's fall from a bicycle, that near drowning event at a friend's cottage, a burn on his hand at a campfire, his broken leg from a fall from a tree, and a concussion from football. She almost smiled because the sorrow of those moments had been overcome by endurance and removed by time, but that moment of relief was temporary. Carla revisited worry about Zeke's presently veiled situation. Her love for Zeke made it difficult to watch him suffer. Then she felt anxiety increasing and encroaching. She deemed herself helpless and afraid, so by default she prayed. *God, I don't have control here. I don't know anything. Help Zeke. Help me. We're in Your hands.* That surrender, that acceptance allowed some calm to return.

At the school, Carla found three police cars and an ambulance on the front lawn. Some students and administrators were speaking with officers. She parked nearby. Just as she exited the car, her phone rang. She hoped Zeke was calling. Instead, it was the principal, Mr. Garrison. "Zeke is with us in the office. He's been a victim of an attack. Paramedics are treating him for some serious bleeding. They plan to take him to North Eutopia Hospital."

"I'm at the school now. I'm coming in to see him," Carla reported. She shoved her phone into her jacket's side pocket while she ran into the front entrance of North Eutopia High School. Garrison greeted and led her to his office, where Zeke received medical attention. He was talking to the paramedics. *He's conscious, thank God. What a bloody mess!* "Zeke, what happened? Are you okay?" *Stay calm. Don't cry. Show him strength.* But Carla could not hold back her tears.

"I'm a little banged up, but I think I did pretty well defending myself. A kid named Jason—he doesn't even go to this school anymore—came at me with a baseball bat," Zeke explained.

Carla pulled a tissue from her purse to soak her tears. "Why?" she asked while paramedics placed him gently on a stretcher.

"You know why, Mom. But there were others there to help me. They got hurt too, but not as bad as me."

"This kid, Jason—what happened to him?"

"He took off. So did his friends." I don't know why he came here today, other than to be with his two racist buddies," Zeke said.

One of the paramedics spoke. "We need to get him to the hospital, ma'am. Would you like to follow us there in your car?"

"I would." Carla wanted to consider further implications, but the shock of Zeke's condition prevented that.

The principal addressed Carla while pointing to an officer who had just entered the office. "I know Constable Rodrigues will want to speak with you and Zeke, and I would too. Is it possible to meet with you later today?"

Work. She looked at her phone for the time. *I have to phone them. This is going to be a long day.* She replied, "Can I phone you when things settle a bit, when I know more?"

"That's fine. After you call, I can arrange for Constable Rodrigues to be here too."

Constable Rodrigues concurred. "No problem. I can interview you here, ma'am, or at the station, when you're ready."

"I'd prefer to talk with you here," Carla confirmed. Rodrigues and Garrison nodded in agreement.

Rodrigues retrieved his notepad and pen. "One of my colleagues tracked down and arrested the main instigator. We're still looking for the other two suspects."

"Thank you, Officer." Carla watched her son leave the office on a stretcher. "And thank you, Mr. Garrison. We'll talk later." She scurried out of the office to close the gap between herself and her son. The principal followed her outside, but he veered toward one particular police officer who was talking to two students. Then a bell rang to indicate a class change.

While Carla waited for the ambulance to leave, she pondered future events. *Can the police provide some kind of protection for Zeke—restraining order or something like that? Please, God. No permanent damage. Heal him. Make my boy whole.*

Who are the other two boys? Are they the same kids as last time? If they are, then they can't be in the same school as Zeke. I want Mr. Garrison, the police, or someone to do something about that.

What if these guys ignore police orders and continue to harass us? Carla considered security systems at home and how soon she could have them installed. *How much do they cost?*

I want to believe I've been a good parent. Right, Zeke? Tell me I've been a good parent. I need to know. Tears again dripped from Carla's face onto the bottom of the steering wheel and onto her sweater. She didn't bother to reach for paper tissue.

As her imagination prepared for what lay ahead, she remembered experiences at the North Eutopia Hospital and other times in hospitals in South Eutopia. To prevent her from not panicking, she transformed them into a set of expected outcomes. Time and good medicine healed. Because his injuries appeared severe, Zeke would receive immediate attention ahead of others in the emergency room. Carla would remain by his side through all procedures, which included x-rays, stitches, casts, bandaging, and scans. He might say with swollen, bruised lips that revealed an unbalanced smile, "Thanks for being here, Mom." He would reach for her hand with exposed fingers that emerged from hardened plaster on his left hand. Zeke might comment, "You missed work today."

Carla would tell him, "For you, it's all worth it." She would pause. She would reciprocate a smile. "What do you say we return to the school and tell Mr. Garrison and the police exactly what happened?"

She imagined Zeke quipping, "Does that mean I can't go to football practice?"

Red lights on the ambulance began to flash, which triggered a latent resentment that crescendoed into rage within Carla. It moved onto the street. As soon as Carla started her automobile, her car radio happened to broadcast an interview with an expert on disciplining children. While she followed the ambulance, she finally processed what Zeke had said. *Jason! Jason and his two racist friends! This Jason is the son of that bigoted bitch in the coffee shop! Why she nuh home with her delinquent son on suspension?* Carla screamed in anger at her radio, "Go tell it to dat loudmouth, Gilda!"

REUNION

NOT ALL PEOPLE enjoyed their high school experience. My buddy Solomon says those were the folks who didn't get involved in sports, yearbook, debate teams, student government, and radio club etcetera. I think he's right. Also, those people usually don't attend high school reunions. I'm sure there are other reasons for absence: commitments, great distances, busy schedules, health, fear of being overshadowed, insecurity about physical appearance, and death. That last one is the best excuse. That's a sure topic of discussion at a reunion: "Do you know who died?"

High school involved romances. Some lasted past graduation. So-and-so dated so-and-so. So-and-so married so-and-so. They divorced. They married too young. Perhaps they didn't really know each other. Perhaps they didn't go to Baskin-Robbins to try out all the flavours. So-and-so married so-and-so, and they're still together. Go figure. Vanilla is a very steady seller.

After Eutopia Memorial High School's fifty-year reunion, one romance budded that none of us in our graduation class expected, but it especially surprised the lovers themselves. Let me elaborate.

Solomon, Raymond, and I attended the reunion together. Raymond, in his usual fashion, had no verbal filters. He practised freedom of thought accompanied by freedom of speech. At the reunion, he said exactly what he thought. Friends found that shocking because they didn't remember Raymond being that way. One person took him to task on that. Fireworks happened, but I'll get back to that.

It's entertaining when it's just us three, but when Raymond's with a larger group, it can be discomforting. Don't get me wrong. He's a good guy. Raymond has a kind disposition and a strong sense of right and wrong. He is a people person. He is loyal. His generosity is quiet and considerable.

However, Solomon was wise to suggest we meet for dinner before the reunion's first evening of events. It was astute also to let Raymond reunite with others without us so that Solomon and I weren't completely embarrassed. We spread out on our own, yet colliding that evening into Raymond with others could not be completely avoided. Solomon's coaching during dinner about employing restraint on Raymond's speech paid off, with one exception.

Twenty-five years earlier, Raymond moved to Dallas to run a business that he purchased, but somehow his marriage dissolved there. He loved to return home to visit his parents and us. Once a year Raymond, Solomon, and I got together to eat and to golf. We would visit his parents too, just like the old days. (Solomon joked with Raymond's mother, "Can Raymond come out to play?") Raymond drank no alcohol. However, Solomon and I have been faithful, fat, beer drinkers. Raymond's been a handy, willing, designated driver when he's come north.

Raymond's appreciation for the old neighbourhood had been a repeated refrain with each visit. He missed home, and details from our maturation lived vividly in his mind. "This was a great place to grow up," he would say. We agreed. Nevertheless, those detailed, unfiltered, often politically incorrect, sexist memories made our eyes roll. He revived teenage male experiences and thoughts from thirty-seven years earlier. It was like time travel for him, but Solomon and I could only observe his journey and offer comment.

At the reunion, Raymond immediately asked, "Malcolm, Brenda Stern's pretty hot, don't you think?" I maintained silence, so he turned to Solomon and repeated, "Sol, look at Brenda. She's still damned good looking, don't you think?"

"She's lovely, Raymond," he replied. "All these women were lovely then, and they're lovely today, almost four decades later. Just like us lovely guys." Solomon massaged his big belly.

Raymond laughed in response. "Come on, you guys. Get into the mood here!" he urged us.

That was my cue to leave. "I've gotta say hi to the administrators here who're hosting the event. I'll see you later," I said while I walked toward the corner of the auditorium. With my time as vice principal at two different high schools in the Eutopia School District, organising reunions has been hard, underappreciated work. Complimenting the principal on a pleasant and successful event and talking about recent events in school board politics mandated a visit.

"Ooh, let's watch Malcolm Reid hobnob with the principal!" Raymond kidded in a town crier voice. "She's hot, Malcolm! Introduce me!"

I didn't look back. After my visit with the principal, I monitored two husbands of classmates of mine who attempted to convince other classmates that they were in grade 12 English together. I knew that they didn't go to our school, but it was entertaining to watch my unknowing classmates squirm because they couldn't remember these husbands in their English class. Such pranksters.

When I ventured in Raymond's direction again, I could hear him announce quite clearly in a small group, "Why didn't we date? I was crazy about you." His bluster reminded me a bit of Rodney Dangerfield's character in *Caddyshack*. I passed that group to visit someone who came from a great distance to attend the reunion. Solomon was talking with her. After university, Andrea Britton left for Hollywood to become a successful writer and director, specialising in comedy. With her stood her second husband, James Raven, the novelist. They held no airs and drank beer with Solomon and me and others. We celebrated their success, and they celebrated ours.

I told you that I would get back to the fireworks. Raymond and Brenda Stern had a loud argument that caught the attention of many in the room, including Solomon and me. We excused ourselves and went to rescue Raymond. Brenda held back no anger. Raymond seemed amused.

Reflecting back on high school days, Brenda had great marks because she studied seriously. She exhibited intelligence constantly. She wore black-rimmed glasses, had black hair, wore no make-up, dressed unfashionably, argued for all underdogs, and projected little typical femininity. She associated with many, but I can't remember her having any close friends. Even Andrea Britton said that she and other girls stayed away from Brenda. "She was strange. All that feminism made us uncomfortable. She was ahead of the curve. I wish I had her with me in Hollywood." Back in high school, Brenda was an individual, a loner, and an idealist.

She started in an academic career, specialising in women's literature as a professor at two universities. However, Brenda escaped scholastic endeavours and veered into capitalism. She found a niche as a consultant in business, starting first in banking. She advised corporations on equity, seeking to change company cultures. With her efforts, she felt she had some success. They rewarded her handsomely for her expertise. She travelled the world not only to convert misogyny into equality but also to champion egalitarianism in the workplace for all people. Somewhere in that time between high school and the reunion, she transformed from a caterpillar into a butterfly.

Her enthusiasm for feminism made her unusual in the early seventies. I couldn't remember anyone in high school dating her. She didn't seem the dating type, and though I respected and liked her, I was not attracted to her. Perhaps other males in Eutopia Memorial High School found her intimidating. Remembrance left the impression she didn't send signals to come hither. She didn't care. She left Eutopia and didn't return—until this reunion.

Raymond had triggered Brenda's wrath by referring to her as a babe and hot. She had "all the right curves in the right places," and she had "preserved" herself well. She no longer wore glasses. In a complimentary, form-fitting dress with cosmetics underscoring her natural beauty, Raymond expressed without nuanced language how stunning she looked. "And I particularly find your intelligence sexy." The gathering giggled, gasped, and guffawed. "What's wrong with me telling you that I find you attractive, that maybe we should get it on?" he argued.

Solomon interrupted, admonishing Raymond in front of our classmates, "Really, Raymond? In front of everyone?" A few laughed at the unintended meaning. That gave licence for others to join the discussion. Solomon held onto Raymond's elbow with both hands to pull him out of the situation. Instead, Raymond shook himself free from Solomon's grasp.

Then Brenda responded with a clear, strong, percussive voice. "You are a dinosaur, Raymond!" Brenda declared with a smile on her face. "What makes you think you're God's gift to women, or that they can be spoken to in that way?"

"It's beyond that, Brenda," Mary advocated. Her husband was one of the two pretending to be graduates. She stared down all the men in the group, including her husband. "Comments about how Brenda looks and her sex appeal are completely inappropriate, whether or not he said them in public or private. Raymond's a misogynist, and apparently he's not ashamed of that." Seemingly enjoying Mary's support of her, Brenda smiled.

"Mary, you wouldn't know a misogynist even if he gave you his business card," Raymond responded. He turned to Brenda. "Is what I said offensive if it's true and truly felt? It wasn't an insult. It was a flattering remark." He stopped to regard disapproval of others. "Guess I stirred a wasp's nest."

"'If I be waspish, best beware of my sting,'" Brenda quoted Shakespeare.

"You must know that I am not a male chauvinist. I support women's rights. I run my company on the principle of equal pay for equal work. I employ people regardless of gender, sexual orientation, religion, or race. People with disabilities are also key to my business's success."

"Do you comment publicly on their appearance?" Brenda volleyed.

"Well, no, but I don't hit on them like I am now with you—in public no less, in front of all our old friends." Raymond turned to Solomon. "It's okay if I told her this in private, right?" Solomon nodded in affirmation. "Sorry. I should have propositioned you privately." The crowd laughed.

Brenda then did something surprising. She advanced toward Raymond, brushing the back of her left hand from his neck to his jawbone. She pulled his head down and kissed him with enthusiasm on his lips. With a coy smile, she commented, "That will give you something to think about." Then she retreated, left the group, and disappeared through the crowd. Exit stage right.

At that moment, the organisers talked over the public address system, announcing the committee that organised the reunion, including some classmates and teachers from that time. We all clapped in appreciation. During that reunion, chats with teachers who attended surprised me. They remembered me. They even told stories about things I did or said in classrooms. I realised they cared about us, and that was why they attended. They still cared.

Solomon and I bumped into each other again. "Where's Raymond?" he asked.

"I haven't seen him since the scene with Brenda Stern." I paused. "Do you think he embarrassed himself and left?"

"Embarrassment doesn't happen to him. But he's our ride home. We'd better find him." Solomon sent me outside to search for him while he investigated inside. It was cooler outside. All those people made the auditorium warm. Outdoors was quieter too. That provided a break, some peace.

In the parking lot, a few people were reunited with their cars, and their headlights blinded me while I located Raymond's rental. It was still in the same spot where we left it when we arrived. Raymond

REUNION

wasn't there. I glanced around the lot, but I couldn't see him. I returned to the venue's entrance and met Glenn Everest and Patsy Van Alstyne in conversation. We exchanged greetings and shared details about our lives. "So why aren't you inside with the crowd?" Patsy asked.

"Oh, I was, but I'm looking for Raymond out here," I replied. Patsy and Glenn laughed. "What's so funny?"

"Raymond and Brenda were making out in the parking lot," Glenn informed.

"Making out" had a wide definition when we were teenagers. It was about acting on a sexual attraction, but it could mean anything from kissing to intercourse. My eyes opened wide. Patsy could see my confusion.

"They were kissing pretty intensely before they got into Brenda's car and drove away," Patsy collaborated. "It was weird. Who'd have thought those two would hook up at the reunion?"

That two opposites who had just argued publicly, who had no romantic history together, who rode to dissimilar places on separate train tracks, found each other with compulsive, passionate attraction ... well, that couldn't quite sink into my brain. Besides, Raymond was our designated driver. Solomon had to know.

"He did what?" Solomon reacted with incredulity. "With Brenda Stern?"

"That's what Glenn and Patsy said."

"They've been drinking," he concluded.

"No, we've been drinking. We need Raymond to get us home," I replied.

"Let's call a taxi. I'm not going to stop their fun," Solomon said. Then he exploded with laughter.

Raymond still returned home annually to visit his mother. His father died two years ago. Solomon, Raymond, and I continued to golf together during his visits. That reunion changed his life. He sold his business in Dallas and moved to Victoria, British Columbia, to live with Brenda Stern.

"Not everyone loves Raymond," Brenda told me, "but I secretly liked him from a distance years ago. He secretly liked me too. Neither of us acted on it until the reunion. We didn't expect romance and love, but it was worth the wait."

They watch whales, identify birds, study insects, keep bees, and grow flowers together. She produces nature videos. Raymond has taken up painting, focusing on nudes, exclusively of Brenda. Now part of a golfing foursome, Brenda plays better than the rest of us. Raymond wants to donate a painting to Solomon and me. We have thanked him, repeatedly declining his offer. Brenda smiles each time.

THE NEW GIRL

AT SIX FEET in height and weighing 190 pounds, it was not easy for Mr. Patel Mehra to hide in a locker. However, he did with uncomfortable success. In the quiet confines of one of his grade 8 portable's lockers, he re-evaluated his decision to find the culprit, the person writing threatening notes to his students. *Why am I doing this? Am I out of my mind? What if a student decides to put a lock on this? I'll look like an idiot. That is if I ever get rescued.*

As a first-year teacher at North Eutopia Elementary School, Mr. Mehra had the daily responsibility of taking attendance of that grade 8 homeroom there, but he taught those students science in the chief science classroom inside the main building. For one period a week, grade 7 students had spelling with another teacher in that portable, but no other classes met there. This lack of classroom use and supervision created opportunities for some abuse by a few students.

Trouble started when a new student moved into the class from another rural community, Saamis, about three hours away. At first, students welcomed her, even invited her to their rural homes, but soon after shunning showed. A series of incidents in the community involving severed horses' tails brought about police investigation. Rumours in the class abounded, and they centred on the new girl from Saamis.

Patel's girlfriend, Nira, asked questions of him in the telling of this story. "Wait. This girl was cutting off horses' tails?"

"I don't know. That's what the kids thought."

Mehra, being a new teacher to the community and a visible minority, had empathy for the new student and wanted others not to jump to judgement. To several students he said, "Give her a break. Just because she's new and the trouble started when she arrived, that doesn't mean she's responsible."

"But Mr. Mehra, she's the one putting all those threatening notes in the lockers. Those threats didn't happen to us; they happened to our horses. When she first got here, a few us tried to be her friend. I don't think she liked us. I'm sure she's responsible for all this because none of us would harm a horse around here, and we all like each other," argued Sandra, away from the ears of other students during science class. "We love our horses. We didn't have this problem before she came."

Mehra thought highly of Sandra. *Maybe she's right.* After inquiries, he learned of no progress of police and administrative investigations, so Mehra chose to investigate on his own.

Nevertheless, Mehra knew that good relationships between him and his students required getting to know each other. In his attempt to know the new girl better, he attempted to converse with her.

"So how has the move here been for you?"

"Okay."

"Have you made any friends yet?"

"No."

"The kids here are good kids. Do you do sports?"

"No."

"Lots of sports in this community. You could make friends that way."

"I don't like sports."

THE NEW GIRL

Mehra did not relinquish hope. "Or the arts: theatre, dance, visual arts, music. You could make friends there."

"I don't like arts. I don't need friends." The new girl walked back to her desk.

Nira commented, "What a cold fish."

Mehra emphasised to Nira one thing: "Yes, but I didn't give up on her."

Those soaked-in-cheap-perfume, menacing notes were in a file in Vice Principal Garrett Vickers's office, and Mehra examined them with Vickers. They scrutinised first the new girl's handwriting from a science test and then the handwriting of all students in the class. Vickers and Mehra, without completely consistent evidence, determined that no student in that class wrote those threats.

"Garrett, could we place a camera in the portable?" asked Mehra.

"A camera's not likely to be approved for a portable, but even if it is, it will take six weeks to be done," Vickers replied. "I can try."

Mehra didn't want to be critical, so he remained silent, and not for the first time about administrative strategic thinking. *How can I properly supervise homeroom attendance in a portable in which I don't teach while being responsible for my science classroom for first period with a different set of students? Shouldn't my homeroom assignment be my first period science class?*

"Patel, if you can figure out this horse tail and notes thing," offered Vickers, "I'll be grateful. The community's quite upset."

Upset? No kidding. So are the students. Who cuts off horses' tails? Why haven't the people doing this been caught? Why haven't they been caught on video somewhere?

Nira interrupted Mehra's story. "So you looked at all the students' writing including the new girl, and none of the writing matched the threatening notes?"

"There were similarities, but we couldn't conclude that it definitely was the new girl putting those notes in kids' lockers. We didn't want to accuse her without solid proof."

With a small laugh, Nira teased, "So now you're a handwriting expert? I think you've got a soft spot for this new girl. Or she's way too clever."

In each instance, the nasty notes appeared in mornings in different individual students' lockers. Custodians locked portables at 4:00 p.m. and unlocked them before 8:00 a.m. Most students came to school by bus, and town kids were about 30 percent of student enrolment. It seemed logical that someone, perhaps a student from town, planted those threats in unlocked lockers first thing in the morning, before arrival of buses, attendance, the national anthem, and announcements. *Then again, it could be a bussed student. I have to solve this now because these students are distressed.*

Mr. Mehra decided to follow the custodian in her morning duty, choosing to hide in a locker in the portable's locker bay, separate from and not visible to the classroom. Perhaps he could learn more and catch the person responsible.

Nira was incredulous. "You hid in a locker?"
Mehra replied, "Yes, in the locker bay inside the portable."
"You are a nutbar."

This was not a bright idea. Quit wiggling. I'm making noise. I wonder if my breathing can be heard. Don't be panicked! What I'm doing could certainly be misconstrued. Oh, here comes someone. The sound of the door opening and closing with footsteps and two voices about three lockers away registered with him. They talked about their families. *They're not passing nasty notes. That's Jessica and Brenda ... not likely them. And I'd be surprised if two or more students were involved, although it's possible ...*

Then reverse order of sounds followed so that he was alone again. *Damn! My shoulder's cramping.* He couldn't even groan because two boys, Phil and Leroy, arrived. They threw a ball of some sort several times against the wall next to the lockers. *So that's why that wall is so marked up.* There was no indication in their conversation about anything nefarious. After about two minutes, they left.

A girl and boy entered, and their conversation centred on a tawdry liaison between two teachers. *I didn't know that. They're right. The amount of time they spend together is considerable. The obvious is always misinterpreted. I've given them the benefit of the doubt. I'm always the last to know these things.* Two or three students joined them. Lockers opened and closed. Then Patel Mehra's phone vibrated without noise. *Damn!* He jerked, and something fell along the wall of the locker onto its floor about the same time as a body slammed into his locker door.

"Why'd you do that?" Mehra recognised the voice of Fred Lemming.

"Do what?"

"Push me into the locker door?"

"Because I felt like it." That voice belonged to Grant Pardin. He began to laugh. Then Fred's body slammed again into the locker door. This time it opened, revealing their teacher's hiding place. Seemingly unaware, Fred and Grant began to grapple, falling to the floor to continue their physical playfulness. Mr. Mehra slowly reached forward to close the locker door while the two boys continued wrestling and laughing.

Another student entered the portable. "What are you guys up to?" It was Sandra.

"Nothing," Grant replied with a snarl. Grant Pardin had been a regular visitor to the office for disciplinary issues. "Why's it your business?" The boys got up from the floor.

Fred had Grant in a headlock. Sandra commented, "What are you doing, Fred, squeezing a zit?" That ended the headlock, but they continued to push back and forth.

Sandra retrieved something from her locker, the one next to Patel Mehra's hiding place. "Don't hurt yourselves," she warned. *Good and reliable Sandra.*

"How can we get into trouble with you around?" Grant responded. "I smell a rat, don't you, Fred?"

"Morons," Sandra retorted. Mr. Mehra heard them all leave for the main building.

Nira jumped into the story. "So this Sandra and the boys didn't see you even though the door came open?"

"She entered the locker bay after I closed the door," Mehra clarified. He sipped his beer. "If the boys weren't wrestling, I'm sure they'd have seen me."

Nira remarked, "Close one."

Alone in the locker, he remained for about ten minutes. He could not scratch itches, his neck cramped, and restlessness arrived. His bladder reminded him of how many cups of coffee he had this morning. Then a stampede of students entered. Some visited lockers, and others walked past the locker bay, probably to sit in their desks on the other side of the wall. The locker bay cleared, and the bell rang. The national anthem played. The sound of students standing for the anthem included shuffling feet, desks moving, whispered conversations, and Grant Pardin asking, "Where's Mehra?"

THE NEW GIRL

He sensed no one in the locker bay, so he exited the locker. *Good. No one's here. No one knows.* He scratched itches with satisfaction. He stretched like a cat, cautious not to make noise as he did so. As announcements began, students returned to their seats, and he appeared at the back of the classroom. A few students noticed his presence, but no verbal reaction followed.

He attempted to take attendance, but his pen was not in his pocket, so he borrowed one from Sandra to do so. He dismissed the homeroom. As they passed the locker bay to exit the portable door, Grant and Fred watched Mr. Mehra examine the door to the locker that Grant had pushed Fred into earlier that morning. His hand brushed over a new dent in the door. Grant and Fred exited sheepishly. Patel opened the door and bent down. There on the locker floor, he recovered his personal pen that had fallen during solitary confinement. *My father's graduation present. I can't lose this.*

During the day when he wasn't teaching, he thought about what he had heard in the morning's stakeout. *I didn't hear anyone doing anything like planting notes in lockers.* Through the day, no threatening notes appeared. *All the class attended today. What happened? Am I supposed to do this again tomorrow?*

Patel Mehra concluded with patience, *Give it time a little more time. This has been going on for almost three weeks. No more hiding in lockers. Whoever's involved will slip up.*

During homeroom the next morning, the new girl received a threatening note, stained with cheap perfume, inside her binder. It was a mess. Mehra took it to Vice Principal Vickers. "Patel, I hoped this stuff would go away, but it hasn't," he complained. "I'll call the police and update them."

Nira interrupted the story. "Patel, what happened with all the horse tail stuff?"

"It stopped by then. No new leads according to Vickers. That allowed the better natures of classmates to accept her. And another funny thing: once the new girl received that threat, the others expressed sympathy and comfort, especially Sandra. However, I noticed that short letter had one unusual characteristic."

Written on standard three-hole lined paper, the left margin was unusually wide and bright pink. *If the new girl is guilty, I wonder if this is an attempt to deflect suspicion away from her.*

During Mr. Mehra's preparation period later that day, he tracked his grade 8 homeroom students to the library where their language arts class worked. All had their binders in front of them on desks. He looked over their shoulders at their lined paper. He asked questions about their work. The fourth student whom he visited had one sheet of the same wide, bright, pink margin on the left side of three-ring lined paper.

"Did you buy that paper, Grant?" Mr. Mehra asked with feigned innocence.

"No. The new girl gave it to me," Grant replied with mild annoyance.

Mr. Mehra continued to visit other students in the class. Again, with the same obvious paper, Leroy responded, "The new girl, she gave it to me."

Two students later, the bright pink left margin surfaced again. Mehra's thoughts went to the movies. *What did Hitchcock call it? The McGuffin? Yes, the McGuffin.* This time Jessica had it. She normally had all the school supplies she needed, but today she needed to borrow paper from … the new girl.

When Mr. Mehra visited the new girl, her binder was full of that bright pink, left-margin, three-hole-punched lined paper. *Bingo.* He asked her for a piece for himself, and she gladly gave him one. He

GROUP WORK

You're not. Thanks for your concern, though." Richard gushed with abundant assurance and charm. The couple seemed sufficiently mollified with Richard's response, so they left. By this point, Nick changed focus of his video recording to Pearl. People around the actors returned to their meals and conversations.

When Marcia's character returned with food, Pearl resumed her complaining. "Why can't I have food? I'm starving. You never feed me!"

A man in his early fifties offered some food to Pearl. "You stay out of this!" Richard told the man. Perhaps fearful, in reaction the intermediary strove to placate Richard, but he would have none of it. Richard stood, posing menacingly with one crutch.

"I'm just trying to help," the man said.

With malice Richard snapped, "We don't need your help, mister." The man visibly cowered.

A mother and her two children stood and walked away with food in hand.

Then Nick abruptly moved forward and spoke in foreign accent, "Sir, you are a bully both to your mother and everyone around you. Stop it." Nick followed with his cell phone, recording the confrontation.

A male voice shouted, "Good. Video the son of a bitch."

A female voice augmented, "Take the video to the cops!" Nick turned around to find where the woman was pointing. He replied to her with a thumb-up with his free hand. At the same time, Richard looked as well, eying a mall security officer entering the food court from the attached security office. Despite this situation being his greatest fear in this academic exercise, Nick remained in role; he had no choice.

If Richard owned panic, he didn't show it. He pointed to the mall security officer for Pearl's sake. He stood, placed his crutches under his arms, and with awkwardness grabbed Pearl's hand, leading her toward the mall security officer. "Come with me, Mother." He released Pearl, and she followed him.

Nick tailed them, now pretending to record on his cell phone. Several people swivelled on their chairs to learn where this drama went next.

Nick pointed to his phone near the face of this approaching mall security officer. Richard inserted himself between Nick and the officer, pushing aside Nick's hand. "Sir, we have something of great importance to tell you," Richard said with imperiousness. "We would like to talk with you in private in your office. Is that possible?"

"Why yes," the officer replied. He pointed to the door that led to the security office. "Come with me." Witnesses to the abuse of Pearl's character stopped their surveillance when the mall official spoke with Richard, so they returned for that moment to concentrate on eating.

Nick, without an accent and in sotto voce, addressed Richard and Pearl, "What are we doing?"

"Play along," Richard answered. Marcia observed from a distance their move, so with food in hand, she headed in their direction. The group trailed the leading officer. Nick put away his cell phone. Then a distressing message over the officer's walkie-talkie halted their steps. A robbery was occurring in the north end of the mall. He bolted.

Richard said to his work group, "Let's pretend to follow him, and then we get out of here."

Having caught up with the other three group members, Marcia added with dryness, "That's too bad. I was going to offer him some fries."

"I'm for disappearing," Nick offered. "Want to meet at my place in an hour?"

Pearl grabbed Richard's arm to hold him back. "We should stagger our exit. Just in case," she suggested.

"Good idea, Pearl," Richard confirmed. Nick and Marcia proceeded ahead of them past the food court into the mall, heading north.

"Hey, I remembered where I've seen you before," Pearl stated.

Richard smiled. "You watch *Ellen*, don't you? And you have for years."

GROUP WORK

"Yes, it was on *Ellen*. I assume it's before you worked construction."

"Actually, both careers overlapped a bit. It was before I married," Richard confessed. "You have a pretty good memory, Pearl."

"So how long were you a Chippendale?" Pearl, with a satisfied smirk, held Richard closely as they scurried arm-in-arm through the food court to the north exit.

At Nick's home, the group watched their video. Pearl reacted strongly when the man who insisted Nick record a video called Richard a son of a bitch.' "Hey, Richard, he wasn't insulting you. He was insulting me! He called me a bitch!" The others laughed.

For the most part, the group remained satisfied with their effort. Richard asked how other members of the group would write about their experience for their professor.

With unexpected emotion that intensified while she spoke, Pearl shared her thoughts. "This course, this assignment, this experience is the best one I've had in university so far. I'll tell you why. First, I played a role in which, for just a moment, that moment when Richard squeezed my arm, when you both denied me food, I got to feel what my sister experienced in her abuse. Before this, I only had sympathy, but because we did this, I reaped empathy." Tears began to flow. She paused to gain back some control. "Second, I met you folks. I feel like we've become friends, and I would like to remain friends with you for the rest of my limited life."

Richard, Marcia, and Nick gazed at each other with bewilderment. Perhaps Pearl's request for friendship triggered memory of Marcia's observation about Pearl's loneliness, so Marcia initiated the group's affirmation. They individually confirmed that they enjoyed working with Pearl and would do so again. Then Richard invited them to see his next performance in two months as Puck in *A Midsummer Night's Dream*. They all agreed to save the date and dine out together after the performance. Pearl beamed at this. Marcia and Richard also smiled when they eyed each other knowingly.

Nick commented next. "It was interesting, to say the least. I don't know if Boal's Theatre of the Oppressed changes anything. None of us are oppressed. Examining our attempt at one aspect of Boal's methods, we made some people in the food court see bad behaviour. Some in the audience expressed consideration for Pearl's character and her circumstance. If those people were touched by this performance, do they change behaviours, personal and societal? I don't know. I doubt it. Did we suddenly stop abuse of elders? No, not at all." Richard and Pearl nodded in agreement.

"Augusto Boal had some success in Brazil and elsewhere. What I learned from this experience is that I'm a coward. I was afraid of being kicked out of the mall, being arrested, and ruining my reputation. I gained a miniscule understanding of the courage and sacrifices others have made to make positive change in this world: Gandhi, Martin Luther King, Susan B. Anthony, Tommy Douglas, Nelson Mandela, Jesus. And yes, I liked working with you all, and I'm grateful to Richard for being such a quick thinker with that security guard. You're a charmer, sir." The others laughed. "And by the way, I figured out where I saw you before."

"You watch *Ellen* too?"

"No. I reset your ankle at the hospital. Remember?"

Richard replied with embarrassment and a chuckle, "Yeah. Now I remember. Of course, yeah." He rubbed his chin. "I agree with you, Nick. Even if we can't measure our effectiveness, the project was worth doing, academically and personally, with all of you. I felt a bit the resentment my character had for Pearl and how needy she was. A little anger swelled up in me. I hope I didn't hurt you, Pearl."

"No, I'm fine." She added with a smile, "You were quite convincing though."

Richard patted her hand. "Sorry, Pearl." She waved away his worry. "In construction, we build structures. This reminded me of renovations. Buildings over time need repair and modernising. What we did today was an attempt at social reconstruction. It was worth doing just to get a hint of what's involved in making change. But I wonder. If we as a society inherently know what's right, why don't we do it? Why don't we change? This just raises more questions for me that I need to research."

Nick interjected. "Save the research, Richard, and listen to me. People don't change because they don't want to. Change happens when we are no longer in control, when change is forced on us."

Richard smiled and continued. "Okay, confession time. I feel guilty about that whole deception thing we did with the mall security guard. My brother was one before he became a cop. I'm thinking about writing that mall security guy's boss a glowing letter. I know mall cops are considered a bit of a joke, but I'm grateful for what they do."

"Don't write that letter, Richard. Really. We're all guilty of deception in this little play. Don't let them know that." Nick turned his attention to Marcia, commenting, "You're pretty quiet, Marcia."

She smiled and took a sip of water. "I've been thinking."

"About what?" Nick asked.

"I'm enjoying this course so far, and I'm glad this worked without us getting arrested. I too want to confess something. I didn't fancy working with you two, Nick and Pearl, because I was worried about preconceptions I had about older people."

Nick recoiled. "I'm not that much older than you."

Marcia clarified, "Yes. You proved that to me. Both of you did. I apologise for prejudging you. Most of all, I'm grateful for this diverse group gelling to accomplish what we did." Marcia paused and smiled. "We learned collectively. This reminds me of why I became a teacher."

Nick raised his glass of water and proposed a toast. "Here's to learning."

"To learning," Marcia echoed. She mimicked his gesture.

Pearl and Richard joined the toast, raising their glasses and clinking them with the rest of the group. In unison they repeated, "To learning."

www.ingramcontent.com/pod-product-compliance
Lightning Source LLC
LaVergne TN
LVHW042244070526
838201LV00088B/8

THE NEW GIRL

asked her, "This is nice paper, and it's good of you to share it. Where did you get it?"

"I don't know. I told my mom that I was out of paper. She brought it home last night."

"You realise that the threatening note you received in your locker this morning was written on that paper?"

The new girl stared at Mr. Mehra without expression or words for a few seconds. "I don't care."

He left the library. *The kids were right. It was the new girl.*

Nira commented, "You figured it out. Good for you. So what transpired next?"

In Garrett Vickers' office, Patel Mehra explained his sleuthing. Vickers lit up with joy at the resolution. He told Patel that he would follow up on this with the new girl, the police, and her parents.

For attendance the next day, the new girl did not show. Several students mumbled about her, but Mr. Mehra's ears could not determine what they said. *I assume she's suspended.* All continued their day without incident. No threatening notes. No missing horsetails. No hiding in lockers. No dropped pens. Only two behavioural issues occurred while teaching, both involving Grant Pardin. *Grant learns the hard way. Oh, well.*

After bus duty and the school emptied of students, Patel visited Garrett Vickers. "So what happened with the new girl?" he inquired.

"It's very strange," Garrett answered. He stared at Patel with bewilderment.

The pause lasted too long for Patel's comfort. "Okay, what happened?"

"They moved. The whole family packed up and moved back to Saamis."

Patel Mehra now knew why Garrett was so incredulous. "What did the police do?"

"I don't know, but they told me that the entire family packed up and moved late last night. They told the police their plans to move back. It's so strange. Oh, well. I didn't have to fill out the suspension paperwork. That's good." Vickers laughed at his own joke.

Mr. Mehra cleaned out the locker belonging to the new girl. With textbooks collected and it now emptied, he found a crushed ball of paper. He unravelled it to find written with scribbling: "I hate it here."

Later that evening, Patel told the story to Nira. "Why did they all move back?" she asked.

"I don't know. I wish I knew. It makes me sad. The new girl needs help. I suspect the entire family needs help. Nothing is resolved. We didn't even get to really know her. There's no closure. I feel like a failure as a teacher."

"You're not. You can't fix the world. You try to make it better. That's all you can do." She held his hand. "I wouldn't want your job even for double your salary," Nira contributed. She gave him a gentle kiss and headed to the kitchen. "Do you want something to eat?"

Patel realised that on an empty stomach, the first beer partially dulled his anguish. More beer would be required. "Sure. Want to order a pizza?" He headed to the fridge to take another one. And again. And again.

GROUP WORK

IT WAS UNUSUAL for a woman at seventy-nine years of age to begin an arts degree, but Pearl Fenchuk no longer coveted conventionality. As a young woman, she had put aside post-secondary education and a career to support her husband in raising children and managing their home, as expected. Pearl looked for new purpose as a recent widow. Her daughter suggested that she pursue a degree. Now, after five years of part-time study, she had three remaining credits to earn. For her next academic conquest, she fancied Eutopia University's night school offering of a cultural studies course on theatre.

When Nick Healy entered the lecture room, he hoped to find a familiar face. He could not. They looked all so young, except for one woman near the entrance whom he assumed was a generation older than him. She reminded him of his mother. Somehow, sitting with the older woman seemed to be the safer thing to do. He reasoned that if the class didn't appeal to him, he could easily retreat out the entrance. She introduced herself. Pearl welcomed him with a smile. While they waited for the professor to appear, Nick and Pearl conversed about weather and their expectations for the class. When the topic of family started, Pearl spoke with excitement about her children and grandchildren. In turn, Nick told her about his three daughters, in particular the oldest one, who was attending her first year of university "thousands of kilometres away." When Pearl asked about her progress, he replied, "I think she's doing fine. At least, that's what she tells me."

Outside and observable from the classroom, at 6:33 p.m., a black pickup truck pulled into the drop-off zone in front of the Beath Arts Building at Eutopia University. From the passenger side, a young man in a cast on his lower left leg hobbled out the front seat. He wrapped a black backpack around himself. Richard Carstairs, dressed fully in black, reached for crutches. He told his wife and two children in the crew cab that he loved them. They said goodbye to each other, and as they left him, the father blew them all kisses from his secure stance. He then entered the building.

Marcia Johnson halted in the entrance to the classroom. She noticed how many younger females were in the room, probably all full-time students who as friends had taken several courses together. Near her, a middle-aged man and an older woman sat separate from the young crowd. She felt it would be safer to sit near them. After Marcia asked Nick if this were the theatre course classroom, he replied, "I believe so. Otherwise we're in the wrong room too." Nick introduced himself and Marcia to Pearl. That was the extent of their conversation because the professor arrived and began her class.

Professor Phyllis Almonberg introduced herself, handing out copies of the prospectus. She talked generally about the expectations of the course. One young student wanted to know the weighting of each assignment. Phyllis replied, "I don't do that. Every assignment is important. I expect all of them to be submitted." She reviewed the reading list for the course, expressing contentment with the number of students who had already begun their readings. A brief introduction to Augusto Boal's guerilla theatre, the Theatre of the Oppressed, followed.

The room presented some logistical problems for the group work she wanted. Desks and chairs loudly announced their unwillingness to move, but through Professor Almonberg's leading and complying efforts of students, groups formed in more circular settings. Yet the younger students' cliquish formations excluded their three older, part-time classmates: Nick, Pearl, and Marcia. Pearl commented, "Well, it looks like just us old folks are going to be working together." Marcia didn't like to consider herself old, but in this setting she was.

Then a stunningly handsome man dressed in black entered the room on crutches. Professor Almonberg confirmed he was in the right course and room. She encouraged him to join a group. Some young ladies in the room had difficulty containing their enthusiasm. Women from two groups chirped, "We can take him." Laughter followed.

"I'm sure you can," the professor inserted. More laughter followed.

Pearl nudged Nick. "He can join our group." Nick smiled. It was then that the young man looked around the room at the various groups. When he saw Nick's welcoming wave to join the older group, without hesitation Richard Carstairs hobbled toward them. Several young women could not hide their disappointment.

Phyllis Almonberg explained their group assignment. Using Augusto Boal's theories, groups had to perform guerilla theatre. She explained what that looked like. Groups would present a social issue to an unsuspecting crowd, using the opportunity to act a planned scenario. Its purpose was to generate awareness of these issues on an unprepared public. Individual written responses of one thousand words on the effectiveness of the project would follow two weeks later. These groups had intensive planning to do.

For the older group, the first few minutes held awkward silences. Conversations sputtered. Things said were not on topic. No one incited much of anything for this group work. Perhaps due to the lack of cohesion among four strangers or complete avoidance of the perception of being the leader arrested the four. Inertia required a push. Realising this, Nick asked for suggestions on social issues. In response, the group exploded with ideas from Marcia and a few from Richard. Addictions, mental health, homelessness, isolation, ageism, family violence, and poverty came forward. However, with Nick as the reluctant leader and Pearl not enthused about those topics (except for some interest for ageism), the two younger group members felt disrespected. Proposals dried up. Then perhaps sparked by discussion about discrimination against older people, Pearl suggested elder abuse.

What was missing in the group dynamic were personal connections, so Marcia used that moment to find them. "Why is this topic of interest to you, Pearl? Have you experienced abuse because of your age?" Marcia inquired with awkward lightness.

"No. I'm well treated by my family, but my sister ..." She paused. Pearl explained that the topic was real, and she would be willing to play an elder's role in a planned but improvised script. Marcia continued with another personal question: "I hope you're not offended by me asking, but I'm curious. Why is a woman your age is taking a cultural studies course?"

"I'm earning my degree, Marcia. Learning should be for life, and I plan to keep living."

"That's impressive. Why now?"

"When I was young, women were discouraged from attending university. I was a wife, a mother, now a grandmother, and soon to be a great-grandmother. Today, I have time to follow my dreams," Pearl shared.

Marcia looked at the others. "Wow. This is good. Do you mind if I ask why all of you are here before we get into this project too far?"

"Why don't you start?" Richard prodded.

Marcia responded, "I teach dramatic arts at Eutopia West High School. I'm taking this course to learn more about this type of theatre, but mostly I need more university courses to move to the next pay category on the teachers' salary grid. So it's not a completely altruistic reason for being here." She grinned briefly. "Besides, I like to think I can still learn even though I've been teaching a few years now. I think it will help me relate more with my students."

Richard Carstairs volunteered next. "I'm here because I need a change of direction, and I think education can assist with that."

Pearl inquired, "What do you want to change, Richard?"

"Construction is good work, but it's hard on the body. If I want to endure or to get ahead in the industry, I need a degree. Maybe it'll lead me right out of construction. I don't know. I wanted to explore what I could do for the rest of my working life. Besides, it won't hurt me to learn. It'll be hard on my wife and kids without me at home as much, at least in the short term, but they've encouraged me in the decision. So here I am." After a short pause, he added, "Oh, and I love theatre. That's why I chose this cultural studies course."

Marcia continued, "Okay. Your turn, Nick. Why are you here?"

With hands clasped together, thumbs resting under his chin with two index fingers over his mouth, Nick replied, "A few reasons. It keeps me sharp. Also, I want to experience again university so that I can compare notes with my daughter. This keeps me current and relevant with her. And I want to learn something not connected to my profession. When I first studied medicine, there was little time for anything else."

Marcia reacted with surprise. "You're a doctor?" Richard appeared puzzled.

"Yes. I have a family practice. Back then I was driven and limited, both personally and professionally. I couldn't learn literature, arts, or social sciences. I appreciated them, but my knowledge was shallow. Finally, at this point in life, I can learn again for the pleasure it provides."

Marcia asked, "Doctors are busy. How do you find time for a class?"

"I make time. Just like exercise."

"Good on you, Nick," Marcia marvelled.

Pearl added, "Good for you too, Richard. But somehow, I know I've seen you before somewhere. I just can't remember."

Richard smiled with a coy look. "I get that a lot. People think they've seen me before, but I look like a type. Maybe I have a doppelganger."

Nick added, "You look familiar to me too. I can't place you." Richard smiled again, relishing his anonymity.

Pearl continued, "I'll figure it out. I'm sure I saw you somewhere."

The professor announced to the class that a fifteen-minute break was commencing. The group disbanded temporarily. Toward the end of the hiatus, several younger female classmates introduced themselves to Richard with vivacity. Marcia observed their interactions. When he returned to the group, she commented, "You have quite a fan club there, Richard."

"Oh, I know. I get that a lot. But I'm married and the father of a boy and a girl." He pointed to his wedding ring. "Most of them back away when I flash this, but for some women, that doesn't stop them. I don't want to continue company with them, so I keep a safe distance."

"You performed admirably, I think—polite, respectful, measured." Marcia reported. "It was interesting to watch."

Reassembled after the break, Pearl took over the focus of the group, returning it to task. She encouraged others to share their personal stories about elder abuse so that the entire group could observe commonalities. Richard, during his teen years, had a neighbour who had been abused by family members. Nick observed a few cases in his practice. Marcia's great aunt had her money and property stolen by a "trusted friend." This propelled Pearl into even more enthusiasm. She praised her group members for their stories, and she suggested roles for each. Richard smiled in reaction and turned to Pearl. "So you want to play a mistreated senior citizen?"

"Yes, I do." She reached out to Richard and touched his knee. "And I want you to play an abusive son."

The two younger members of the group expressed concern about playing roles. Both Richard and Marcia had experience in theatre. "Stanislavski's Method can really mess with the mind if it's not employed properly," Marcia commented as a dramatic arts teacher. "Getting into role sometimes makes it difficult to get out of role. We need to be careful, people."

"When I'm acting, I really commit to my roles," Richard warned. "I don't want to scare anyone, especially you, Pearl. You should have seen me in *Our Town* as Simon Stimson, and in *Jesus Christ Superstar*

I played Judas Iscariot. I was intense. Of course, they were two different types of intensity. Maybe that's where you saw me, Pearl, in the theatre."

Pearl said, "I don't think so. I haven't seen those plays."

"Maybe you saw me in another play," Richard replied.

Nevertheless, despite the cautions, Pearl pushed her idea forward with enthusiasm. The group split into two conversations at the same time. Richard and Marcia expressed concerns to each other. The older two made some decisions for the group on their own. Pearl announced to the other two, "Nick agrees to film it. Now, where do we perform this?"

Richard suggested the shopping centre food court as a good place for an unsuspecting audience. Nick disliked that idea. Legal implications and people's potential reactions concerned him. Debate followed. No other propositions for location emerged.

Pearl pushed forward. "Look. We're running out of time. We can't waste all this time we've used. Look at the deadline. There's not much time left in this class. We all have busy lives. Planning things new will take time outside of class—immediately. This group needs commitment." Pearl paused. "I'm going to read more fully about how Boal's guerilla theatre promoted consciousness and changed things, but potential for change excites me. Let's go to the shopping centre. Let's put on a show the people there won't know is a show. Let's change behaviours, raise awareness. Come on, you guys—show a backbone. What are they going to do, throw a woman in her eighties in jail? I'm willing to take the risk." Nick looked sheepish.

Marcia chipped in, "Well, you're right, Pearl. Success in theatre is often about risk."

Turning to Richard, Pearl asked, "You'll play my abusive son, right?"

"It's not a role I cherish, but I can do it," returned Richard. "I hope I can turn it off. I can be intense, even in improvisation."

Pearl continued. "Nick will be the one who chastises you for elder abuse. He'll try to stir up the people around us. What do you see your role as, Marcia?"

"I could be your abusive daughter," Marcia contributed. "Two abusive children in teamwork together," she said with an exaggerated, iniquitous smirk and posture, performing for Richard. "I can play nasty too." In reaction, Richard chuckled.

Nick commented, "You know, Marcia, you could pass for Richard's sister."

"Go on!"

"I can see it in your faces," he added.

Pearl led further. "Okay, now we have our roles. Nick, we have to make your filming look natural. Why are you filming there?"

Nick suggested, "I'll play a tourist who is creating a short video to show the food court to others back home. Then the abuse grabs my attention. Then the filming changes focus to Nick and Marcia's abuse of Pearl."

"Oh, I like that," Pearl assured the others. "That could be quite natural if we time it properly."

"I don't mean to be overly cautious, and we have spoken superficially about this, but what about permission? Don't we need to get that from mall officials?" Nick asked. "Pearl, I appreciate your sense of adventure, being willing to go to jail and all, but others here have to consider their day jobs."

"You've got the safest role of all, Nick," Pearl reassured.

"Yes, I suppose I do."

Richard deepened commitment. "Permission? I thought this was supposed to be guerilla theatre, Theatre of the Oppressed! We can't let people know what's happening. What if the mall doesn't give us permission? No, to make this work, it must remain a secret. We should be cautious about how close mall security is to our performance. We'll have to leave the food court as soon as we've completed our scene."

With Pearl's leadership, elder abuse became the group's social issue worthy of guerilla theatre. Details of the plan continued, and group members shared complete contact information. However, when they left the class, Marcia and Richard conversed in private while they left the building.

Expressing his doubts about the group work so far, Richard confided to Marcia, "Here we are, more experienced in acting and theatre, taking direction from theatrical novices about a form of rebel theatre. I'm not sure about this."

"I share your concern. This is flimsy. Yet in an improvisation, essential ingredients are risk and trust. We need to remind ourselves about trust, perhaps more than we'd like. It'll work out, Richard."

"Remember when Pearl expressed interest in ageism, but it didn't go anywhere? Then she pushed elder abuse, yet she said she's not abused. What's up with that?"

Marcia paused before she answered him. "I think she's lonely."

Their apprehensive approach to the food court at the mall signalled their primary anxiety about their project: getting in trouble. After scanning the area for absence of mall security, being sure of logistical seating arrangements, and feeling somewhat secure that they could begin, Nick left first to acquire food. Marcia claimed an empty table with four seats near other diners. Richard and Pearl waited outside the eating area for their appropriate moment to play their roles.

Establishing his character, Nick approached Marcia with a tray of food in hand, requesting in a foreign accent if he could join her to eat at her table. She, with loud and inhospitable voice, told him, "No, you can't. My mother and brother are sitting there." She then made a face showing her disgust. This did not go unnoticed. Nick then turned to two people next to Marcia's table, requesting to eat with them. They readily agreed, so he set down his tray of food on their table.

On their journey across the food court, Pearl and Richard conversed in character with excessive volume. Twice Pearl, feigning inattention, bumped into people seated at tables eating. Richard would apologise to them for her, but at the same time he publicly chastised her. Even with two crutches under his arms, he pulled her away with force while she attempted to converse with the people whom she just had nudged. Their loudness and Richard's bullying could not escape observation from people in the court. After leaving those two tables, snippets of conversations about Richard and Pearl rippled around them. Their enlarged improvisations captured an audience. Then Pearl and Richard joined Marcia. Pearl, in character, declared in shrill, discontented voice what food she wanted. Heads turned.

In equally booming voice to reinforce hearing loss for Pearl's character, Marcia declared that her mother didn't deserve food. Pearl whined about being hungry, but Marcia walked away to order food from KFC. Mother stood to complain, "I want some food. I'm hungry!"

From a distance, Marcia turned around and with incrementally increased volume announced, "Shut up, Mom!" At that point, Marcia wondered if she had overdone it, perhaps turning this drama into a comedy, its theatricality too obvious for the audience. She chose to continue, hoping that the patrons of the food court would judge their presence as uncomfortable reality.

From his seated position, Richard's character gripped with strength the mother's arm to yank her down to her seat. Richard leaned into her to tell her something discretely. Pearl's character yelled, "Stop it! You're hurting me!" Richard continued to hold on and talk quietly to her. "I can't hear you! You're hurting me!"

"Stop it, Mom!" Stop it!" was his reply. "You're embarrassing us." One couple left their table with trays and garbage in hand. They glared at Richard as they approached. "Now calm down." He released his grip on Pearl.

The couple asked Pearl if everything was all right. Nick stood up to take a video of the food court.

"He's hurting me, and they won't give me food!" Pearl protested.

"She's just being belligerent," Richard responded. "Don't worry about Mom. We've got this under control. We're used to her outbursts.